Ali stepped into Taylor's arms

He hesitated, feeling a surge of nerves. It wasn't that he didn't want to hold her, to feel her curves pressed up against him as they danced to a bluesy number. It was that he wanted it too much.

Ali was aware of Taylor's uneasiness, but she assumed it was merely his embarrassment over his dancing. "Look, it just takes practice. Why, before I'm through, I'll have women falling all over you."

Every woman but her, that was. Ali had to keep her distance. Which wasn't easy when she was tight against his lean, very appealing frame. Instead of her teaching Taylor the fox-trot, *he* was teaching *her* that her body could go haywire close to his. So she extricated herself from his hold.

A slow torch song came on. Taylor held his arms out. "One more before we say good-night? Just to see if I'm catching on?"

Something told her that Taylor was catching on fast. Maybe faster than she could handle. . . .

Dear Reader,

Laughter and romance is a combination that has always hit the spot for me. Ever since I was a kid, I've had a love affair going with the marvellous screwball romantic films of the thirties and forties. The greatest fun and challenge for me has been to capture the humor of those movies and transplant them into contemporary romance novels. In the ten Temptation stories I've written to date, I've had a chance to let my madcap imagination run wild, combining lighthearted romance with some good old-fashioned slapstick.

The Fortune Boys series, in particular, is my loving tribute to all those bygone romantic comedies I adore. In these four books, I've taken each of four brothers in turn, all dyed-in-the-wool bachelors dripping with money, celebrity and success, and teamed them with four classy women with spirit, spunk and passion to spare. What happens after that is strictly chemistry, but I'll leave you to discover the outcome.

I hope you have enjoyed #412 *Adam & Eve,* #416 *For the Love of Pete,* #420 *True Love* and #424 *Taylor Made.*

Sincerely,

Elise Title

P.S. I'd love to hear from my readers.

TAYLOR MADE

ELISE TITLE

Harlequin Books

TORONTO • NEW YORK • LONDON
AMSTERDAM • PARIS • SYDNEY • HAMBURG
STOCKHOLM • ATHENS • TOKYO • MILAN
MADRID • WARSAW • BUDAPEST • AUCKLAND

Published December 1992

ISBN 0-373-25524-1

TAYLOR MADE

Prologue

"WILL YOU PLEASE STOP fussing over me, Doris."

"You listen to me, Nolan Fielding. You may know all there is to know about lawyering, but when it comes to looking after yourself, you're still wet behind the ears." Doris Lester stood over her boss, holding out two tablets in the palm of her hand.

The seventy-two-year-old attorney, a big ruddy man with cropped graying red hair, plucked the cold pills from her hand. She poured him a glass of orange juice, extending it in his direction after he deposited the tablets into his mouth. He grimaced as he swallowed them.

"There," he said petulantly. "Do you feel better now?"

"No. But *you* will."

Nolan Fielding smiled wryly at his secretary. It was a typical Doris response. Somehow, she always managed to get in the last word. He leaned back slightly in his chair, observing her as she straightened up his desk. She was sixty-four years old, small and pleasant looking in an unobtrusive way, with a slim, modestly proportioned figure. What one noticed about her, however, was not so much her appearance as her character. Doris Lester was strong-minded, outspoken, and unendingly loyal. She had come to work for him straight out of secretarial school and they had been together ever since— nearly four decades—the bachelor lawyer and the spinster secretary. Odd, how in all those years together, he had never given her much more than absentminded notice. Odder still, that lately he'd found himself becoming more aware of her....

"It was a particularly lovely wedding," Doris commented as she checked to make sure all his No. 2 pencils had fresh points.

"Yes. A lovely wedding," Nolan Fielding muttered. He slowly shook his head in wonder. Yesterday, he and Doris had attended their third Fortune wedding in less than two years—first Adam Fortune and Eve, then Peter Fortune and Elizabeth, and now Truman Fortune and Sasha. Each wedding had made headlines. The Fortune brothers, heirs to the vast Fortune's Department Stores empire, were big news. They got to be bigger news with each subsequent wedding—thanks in large part to a unique variation on a tontine that their father, Alexander Fortune, had included as a codicil to his will. In a traditional tontine, a group of people contribute equally to a prize that ultimately is awarded in its entirety to the surviving member of the group. In Alexander Fortune's version, the prize—all the shares in the Fortune stores, which upon Alexander's death were divided equally among his four sons, Adam, Peter, Truman and Taylor—would remain in their possession as long as they remained bachelors. Any of his sons who chose to marry would be required to turn his shares over to his single brothers, thus relinquishing all his interest and profits from those holdings. In other words, each of Alexander's sons would be forced to choose either *fortune* or *love*. Thus far, much to the glee and profit of the media, and the delight of their grandmother, Jessica, three of the four brothers had chosen love. Now there was only one Fortune bachelor left: Taylor Fortune, the youngest son....

"She looked remarkably radiant," Doris said offhandedly as she brushed a filament of dust off her boss's pipe rack. While he no longer smoked, thanks to her relentless entreaties, Nolan Fielding liked to keep his old pipes on display as a fond reminder of more carefree times.

"The bride?" Nolan smiled. "Yes, Sasha did look quite beautiful. A striking contrast from that dour Russian comrade who appeared on Jessica's doorstep that first day."

"Oh, yes, Sasha made a beautiful bride." Doris hesitated. "But I was referring to Jessica Fortune," she said, casting him a quick glance. "I suppose, what with the marriage of her third grandson and hearing the news that Eve was pregnant, which will make her a great-grandmother for the first time, she had every reason to glow."

Nolan Fielding snickered. "That wasn't why she was glowing. And you know it as well as I do. The woman has gone dotty over that doctor, Ben Engel, she met in Chicago when she went off to play matchmaker for Peter and Elizabeth last year. Did you see the way the two of them were dancing? And how she kept batting her eyes at him all through the wedding service? And at her age. It's positively—"

"Romantic," Doris finished with a smile. "Just because you're jealous—"

"Jealous? Jealous? Are you saying that I'm jealous?" he blustered.

Doris's smile deepened. "Don't tell me you're having trouble with your hearing now, Mr. Nolan?"

He gave her a sharp look, but then his features softened. "All right," he admitted. "I suppose nothing has ever gotten past you in your entire life, Doris Lester. I admit it. There was a time when I might have been a bit—just a bit—jealous. But, what with all the crazy business going on since that fateful day nearly two years ago when I read the codicil to Jessica's son, Alexander's, will, I've been far too wound up and distraught to think about such foolishness. Besides, I'm not at all pleased by Jessica's meddling in the affairs of her grandsons."

"I would say it was Alexander who meddled first," Doris pointed out. Doris had always been one to speak her mind, even though she knew perfectly well that Nolan had not only been Alexander Fortune's lawyer for almost thirty years, but his good friend, as well. Nolan had helped Alexander get his first store here in Denver off the ground, and his sound advice and encouragement had contributed to Fortune's becoming one of the largest upscale department-store chains in the country—the largest in the Northwest.

"I never did approve of that tontine. Not that I didn't understand Alexander's reasons," Nolan mused. "I believe he truly thought he was protecting his sons from making the same mistakes he'd made when it came to the opposite sex. Four disastrous marriages might well leave a man feeling more than a bit disillusioned about the state of holy matrimony."

"I think the tontine was a terrible idea. Cutting his sons off from their inheritance if they married—it was positively heartless."

"Really, Doris. Alexander wasn't being an ogre. He adored his four sons. You know that as well as I. He honestly felt that the boys would be better off remaining bachelors. He meant to save them the heartache, the financial and emotional stresses, the suffering—"

"What he would have done, had his disreputable tontine been as successful as he'd hoped, was to deprive Adam, Peter and Truman of the blissful happiness they're now enjoying," Doris retorted, cutting him off.

Nolan opened his mouth to argue, then shut it. For one thing, he had long ago learned never to argue with Doris, because she was nothing if not tenacious and always won in the end. For another, he had to admit Doris was right. Adam,

Peter and Truman all did seem to be basking in wedded bliss. It was still too early to tell how Truman would fare on his own financially, but as for Adam and Peter, they'd done remarkably well since giving up their stock in Fortune's for love and marriage.

It still made Nolan chuckle to think that Adam, once an irascible playboy, and his wife, Eve, had become nationally renowned arbiters in labor-management disputes. Over the past two years they had been responsible for keeping many a company from having to contend with a costly walkout or strike. They made a unique team; Adam coming from the management end, Eve from the labor end. Their respective backgrounds enabled them to see both sides of an issue, and each party in a dispute invariably felt they were given a fair hearing and a fair shake. Until recently, Adam and Eve had traveled a great deal and spent much of their time living out of a suitcase, but had settled in Denver now that Eve was pregnant.

As for Peter Fortune—whose fortuitous meeting with his wife, Elizabeth, had centered around a homburg—he, too, was doing exceedingly well without his inheritance. Shortly after his marriage, he opened a small haberdashery boutique in Chicago where Elizabeth practiced as a neuropsychiatrist. The business community had had a big laugh. Hats, they all declared, were passé. Certainly a boutique featuring only hats was pure folly. They'd concluded that within the year Peter Fortune would lose his "homburg." Well, sixteen months and four haberdashery boutiques later, Peter ended up with the last laugh. He was known among the fashion-industry giants as the man who brought not only the homburg, but hats of all varieties back into vogue for men and women. The *Wall Street Journal* had just run a lengthy article on him and his hats were featured in every magazine from *GQ* to *Harper's Bazaar*.

Nolan Fielding had little doubt that Truman, too, would succeed without benefit of the family fortune. He and his Russian wife had big plans to bridge the gap between East and West. At the wedding yesterday, Tru had told Nolan that he and Sasha wanted to start by opening two shops, one here in Denver, importing Russian-made goods, and one in Moscow, featuring inexpensive American merchandise—everything from Frisbee disks to American-flag salt- and pepper shakers. With American fast food doing so well there, it was a good hunch that other American merchandise would be equally as popular. While a venture of this sort wasn't easy, both governments were very amenable to helping the pair in gratitude for their part in bringing to justice not only one but two international smuggling rings. Yes, Nolan mused, Tru and Sasha would certainly succeed at anything they set their minds to.

So now, there was only Taylor left. Taylor—the shy, sweet, most unassuming of the boys—was the sole owner of Fortune's. Unless...

"You look a bit drowsy," Doris remarked, shaking Nolan from his musing. "It might be a good idea for you to take a nap. There's nothing on your calendar until three this afternoon."

"I'm feeling perfectly alert," Nolan retorted. Then, after a short pause, he uttered vaguely, "I was just thinking about Taylor."

"You're worried that he might marry, too."

Nolan sighed. "I could feel their eyes on me all during the wedding—Adam, Peter and Tru."

"Nonsense," Doris said.

"Oh, it's true. And they were all thinking the same thing. That if Taylor were to get married, leaving no other bachelor sons to carry on as Fortune's heirs, then all stocks in the company revert to me, thanks to the final contingency in Alexander's tontine—a contingency I feel certain he never dreamed would be even a remote possibility. As if I want the stocks. As if I need them. I have a perfectly satisfactory sum of money put aside for my old age."

Doris bit back a smile. Considering that Nolan Fielding's seventy-third birthday was just around the corner, she couldn't help but wonder at what age he would consider himself old. Granted, the man was quite fit other than this little cold, which she intended to see didn't turn into pneumonia; and even with a runny nose, the man didn't look a day over sixty-five. He still practiced law, although he'd cut back on his hours—not because he was lacking in energy but because he wanted more time on the golf course.

"Well, don't worry, Mr. Fielding. Taylor Fortune isn't likely to get married. Why, I don't think he's ever even had a serious girlfriend. He's terribly awkward around women. I don't think he danced once at his brother's wedding yesterday. As usual, he spent most of his time doodling—"

"It isn't idle doodling, Doris. The boy happens to be an inventor. All right, I will admit certain of his inventions haven't fared well...."

"You mean like his automated car jack that worked so well it actually flipped the car over? Or his 'robotic handmate,' as he called it, designed for answering phones when both of your own hands are busy? If you remember, he insisted I try that one out myself, thinking it would be the perfect accessory for the busy secretary. Let's see. The first time I used it, the robot hand did lift up the receiver, but instead of depositing it next to my ear, dropped it into my mug of coffee. The second time, it got to my ear, all right. Nearly knocked it off my poor head."

Nolan Fielding chuckled. "Yes, that little gadget did have a few kinks in it."

Doris laughed, too.

"He is a sweet boy, though," Nolan mused, always having had a particular fondness for Taylor.

"He's not a boy, Mr. Fielding. He's thirty-three years old. Nearly thirty-four. And now that he's responsible for running the Fortune's empire, I do hope he's going to be able to put all this gadget nonsense aside."

"According to Jessica, he's planning to do no such thing. He's turned the president's office at the Denver store here into a lab and claims to be on the brink of perfecting his robot household helper that he's been working on for the past two years."

"Oh, dear. Not Homer! I thought he'd given up on that one. If Taylor's robotic hand caused the mayhem it did, can you imagine what disaster an entire robot of his might wreak? I do hope he won't bring it here for us to try out."

Nolan Fielding smiled. "Now, now, Doris. If the robot works, it could be a major boon to the housewife. They all laughed at Thomas Alva Edison and Alexander Graham Bell, too."

Doris looked at him dubiously, but then she smiled, as well. "Stranger things have happened, I suppose." She absently smoothed back her hair, which she wore in a tidy Buster Brown cut, aware that her boss was regarding her in a vaguely different way. She couldn't quite figure out what was behind his expression, but she found it unsettling. When she stopped smiling, this seemed, to her astonishment, to have a direct effect on him. He looked . . . disappointed. No. Surely she was imagining things. She was aware, though, that he didn't avert his gaze. She began to worry that something was wrong. Perhaps those cold tablets were producing some unexpected side effect. . . .

Nolan Fielding did feel a bit odd, but he doubted it had anything to do with cold tablets. "Do you know something, Doris?"

She gave him an apprehensive look. "Do I know what, Mr. Fielding?"

"Two observations, actually," he found himself saying. "One is that in all the forty years you've worked for me, you've never once called me by my given name."

Doris looked astonished. "Your . . . given name?"

"Nolan, Doris. My given name is Nolan."

Doris was flustered—an uncommon experience for her. "Yes. Of course, I know your given name. It's just . . . Well, a secretary doesn't go about calling her employer by his . . . given name. It isn't respectful."

"Really, Doris. After forty years, wouldn't you grant that we've gone a bit over the border of strictly employer and employee?" He flushed, but nonetheless held her gaze. For the life of him, he couldn't imagine what had come over him. But having started on this unexpected course, he found he had no inclination to detour from it.

"If you mean . . . do I consider you as . . . more than merely an . . . employer—" His grin brought her up short. "Are you making fun of me, Mr. Fielding? Because if you are . . ."

"I am most definitely not making fun of you, Doris," Nolan Fielding said with a fervency that surprised them both.

"I don't think you're yourself today, Mr.—" But somehow she couldn't bring herself to say, Fielding. Not that she could imagine calling him Nolan, either. Really, this was a fine how-do-you-do.

"Aren't you curious about my second observation, Doris?"

Curious though she might be, she wasn't about to admit it. "I think you could do with a good nap," she said firmly. But the nervous flutter in her stomach colored her tone of voice.

"My second observation, Doris, is that you have a very nice smile."

Doris was flabbergasted. "Really, Mr.—" She hesitated, feeling the heat rise in her cheeks. "Really...Nolan."

Nolan Fielding smiled mischievously. "Yes. Really, Doris."

1

"EUREKA!" THE PIERCING cry came from behind the closed door of the Fortune president's office.

The next moment the door flung open. Taylor Fortune, his chestnut hair practically standing on end, his shirttails half hanging out of a pair of well-worn work pants and his cardigan sweater misbuttoned so that he had a slightly lopsided look, burst into the outer office. He was flushed, out of breath, barely able to contain himself. "He works!"

"He?" Cal Morgan, a VP in the marketing department who'd been called up to a meeting by the new Fortune's president, blanched as he glanced into the open office. Only a few months back when he'd been at a meeting with the previous president, Truman Fortune, the large corner office had been an opulently appointed space done to perfection by one of Denver's top interior decorators. The office now looked like a carbon copy of Dr. Frankenstein's laboratory. Cal Morgan half expected to spot Frankenstein's monster rising from the metallic debris strewn about a long wooden worktable that now resided on the spot where a majestic custom-crafted cherrywood desk had previously sat.

"Homer," Taylor said excitedly, feeling around in his pockets for his glasses only to have his secretary, Rhonda, discreetly point out that they were propped on top of his head.

"Homer?" Cal Morgan repeated.

Taylor slipped his glasses back on and reached for a file on Rhonda's desk. "Homer, my robotic device that can be programmed to do all the basic household chores. Everything from changing the linens to washing floors. Oh, there are still a few minor kinks, but I tell you this little baby is going to be the hit of the Fortune's chain."

A low groaning sound emanated from his office and all eyes turned in that direction. The groan died down, but a moment later there came a high-pitched whine. Taylor frowned, tapping his index finger against his lips, and muttering as he returned to his office, "Like I said. Just a few kinks."

He was about to close the door when he turned back to Cal. "I'm putting everything I've got into financing and marketing Homer for the chain, Morgan. I'd like a preliminary marketing plan from your people as soon as possible." He started to close the door, then paused, beaming ingenuously at both Cal and Rhonda. "The wonders of modern science. Isn't it just great?"

"Great," they both echoed like dutiful employees, giving each other incredulous looks after Taylor closed his office door.

TAYLOR FORTUNE KNEW something was up as soon as he entered his grandmother's parlor and discovered Adam, Peter and Tru sitting there with Jessica.

Jessica smiled at her youngest grandson. "Isn't this a pleasant surprise?"

Taylor eyed his brothers and grandmother. "I'm not sure. Is it?"

Before Jessica could respond, Adam broke in. "Cal Morgan phoned me and told me about your plan to do a marketing blitz on…Homer. Morgan was justifiably concerned."

"And you were concerned enough to get Peter here from Chicago and Tru all the way from Moscow?" Jessica asked Adam.

"I had to be back here for business anyway," Tru quickly replied.

"I see," Taylor said slowly.

Adam cleared his throat. "Look, Taylor, the business is in your hands now. We've got no say. We're just here as brothers who care about—"

"It's a risky venture," Peter broke in.

"Especially as Morgan told me you still have some serious . . . kinks to iron out in Homer," Adam added.

"And even if you do iron them out," Tru interjected, "there could be problems down the line. Or it might not be the hot item you expect and you'd end up having to pull it from the shelves. A big investment in the—in Homer might put you in the hole, Taylor. It could also affect the reputation of Fortune's."

Taylor's expression was thoughtful but noncommittal as he listened to his brothers' arguments. Then, slowly, he turned to Jessica. "What do you think, Gran?"

"I think you're running the show, dear. And I also happen to think Homer might be a big draw for Fortune's."

Adam, Peter and Tru gave their grandmother dismayed looks. Before any of them could argue with her, she waved them off with her hand. "I will say that I wouldn't leave the promotion to someone like Cal Morgan, Taylor."

"You wouldn't?"

"No," Jessica said firmly. "The man lacks vision. As, I'm sorry to see, do your brothers here."

All three in question started to argue against their grandmother's assessment, but again Jessica made a dismissive gesture with a flick of her hand. "Knowing how busy you've been," she continued addressing Taylor, "I took it upon myself to make some inquiries. I wanted to see if there was someone around town who had the imagination, energy, daring and inventiveness to promote Homer in a way that would make the robot a surefire winner."

"And you found someone who fit the bill?" Taylor asked eagerly.

Jessica nodded enthusiastically. "Yes. You might say I found someone 'Taylor made' for the job. The perfect woman."

"Woman?" Adam, Peter and Tru didn't say the word in unison but close to it. And all three were immediately on guard, each of them instantly assuming Jessica had yet another matchmaking plan afoot. While none of them had any complaints at all about her previous matchmaking activities, they all had good reason not to want to see Taylor follow in their footsteps down the aisle. Taylor was the last Fortune bachelor. If Jessica was as successful a matchmaker with Taylor as she had been with them, the family business would be totally removed from Fortune hands, ending up, instead, in the feeble grasp of Nolan Fielding.

"I don't know," Taylor said dubiously, oblivious to the anxieties of his brothers. "I think a man might be—"

"Homer's a device for the homemaker, Taylor," Jessica interrupted. "And most homemakers are still women. And separate from sex . . ."

"Sex?"

"The female sex versus the male sex," Jessica explained with a smile.

"Oh. Right," Taylor said.

His three brothers groaned. "Don't you see the writing on the wall, Taylor?" Tru argued.

"It's a setup," Peter added.

"She's come up with some gorgeous heart-stopper who you're going to find irresistible," Adam warned.

"Nonsense. I picked her because she's the best in the business. And it's strictly business I'm thinking about."

The three married Fortune boys gave their grandmother dubious looks.

She scowled. "You're all behaving like children. Furthermore, you give me far too much credit for your blissfully happy marriages. If I recall—and my memory is still quite good, thank you—none of you fought very hard against falling in love or popping the question."

None of them could truthfully argue her point. Not that this altered their suspicions that their wily grandmother was once again up to her old bag of tricks.

"Who is this woman?" Tru finally asked.

"Yes, who is she?" Peter and Adam echoed.

Taylor, who'd thought of a new idea for solving a minor glitch in Homer, was only half listening as he scribbled some notes on his pad.

"Ali Spencer," Jessica announced.

"Ali Spencer?" Tru echoed.

"Not the Ali Spencer from the Chester Public Relations Agency here in Denver?" Peter asked.

"That hotshot ex-New Yorker you used to promote the Quint line of cosmetics?" Adam said to Peter.

"That Ali Spencer?" Peter asked Jessica.

Jessica nodded. "Yes. If I recall, you thought she did a top-notch job. And she's done some other PR work for Fortune's in the past, always with great success."

Peter grinned. "Ali Spencer."

Adam was grinning, too. "Perfect."

"Perfect?" Tru repeated, bewildered.

Both Adam and Peter nodded. "Not to worry," Adam said, relaxing. "Taylor couldn't be in better hands."

Taylor was surprised by his brothers' sudden shift of attitude. "I couldn't?"

LATER THAT EVENING, after Jessica had gone to bed and Taylor had returned to his carriage house on the grounds to iron out the remaining kinks in Homer, Adam and Peter had the chance to tell Tru why they weren't worried about the prospect of wedding bells for Taylor.

"Don't get me wrong," Peter was saying. "She's not bad looking. And I think she's got a decent figure—although to tell you the truth, she always seemed to move so fast I never got a close enough look at her to be sure. She's as New York as they come. Fast-talking, fast-moving, slick as all get-out, and a real ace schemer when it comes to PR work."

Adam grinned. "Poor Taylor. One encounter with her and he'll be running for the hills."

"And let's face it," Tru added. "As great a guy as Taylor is, I seriously doubt from your description of Miss Spencer that she goes for the shy, retiring type."

"He does have a quirky innocence that a woman like Spencer could take advantage of," Peter remarked with a note of concern.

"On the positive side," Tru interjected, "maybe he'll be so intimidated by her, he'll tell her to forget about the whole deal and hold off on Homer."

"Or maybe she'll take one look at Homer and she'll tell Taylor to forget it," Adam said, ending on what all the brothers considered an optimistic note.

TAYLOR WAS ADJUSTING one of his robot's rotary arms the next morning when there was a series of rapid-fire knocks on his office door. Before he could set down his wrench, the door flew open.

"No one was in the outer office so I figured I'd just announce myself. Ali Spencer." A slender hand shot out, but Taylor was slow on the take, so she dropped it again, all in the matter of a split second. "You must be Taylor Fortune.

And this must be Homer. Catchy name. I like that. Did you come up with it yourself? Yeah, I bet you did. So, when do we start the ball rolling?" She spoke in rapid-fire fashion and her voice had an up-all-night rasp.

Taylor lifted his glasses, his hazel eyes trying to take in the whirling dervish who'd just burst into his office. He saw the pert nose, the chocolate brown eyes, the unruly mass of copper-tinted curls that capped her head. She reminded him a bit of the cartoon character, Annie. From the neck up. However, Taylor found nothing cartoonish about Ali Spencer from the neck down. The effect of her shapely five-foot-seven figure encased in the classy, form-fitting cherry red suit and black suede pumps was serious sizzle.

"Would you . . . like me to give you a . . . demonstration of what he can do?" Taylor asked self-consciously.

She laughed as she eyed the metal robot, then swung her gaze over to Taylor. She had a decidedly sexy, X-rated laugh.

"Hey, shouldn't we get acquainted first?"

Taylor felt his cheeks warm, but Ali merely squeezed his shoulder. "I'm a terrible tease. You'll have to live with it. I can't do anything about it."

Her casual touch produced an instant and unexpected rush of disturbing sensations in Taylor. He jumped back, nearly sending Homer, who was stretched out on the table, onto the floor. It was Ali's quick move that kept the robot from tumbling. She observed Taylor closely as he fumbled for his glasses.

"Oh, well... My brothers are teases, too. Well...not Pete so much, but Tru. And definitely Adam." He wished she'd stop staring at him. He knew he was making an ass of himself.

"Ah, yes. The infamous brothers who all gave up their fortune for love. Great copy." She stepped closer to him. "And you're the last bachelor of the lot, huh? The last real

Fortune man. Hey, I like that. The Fortune Man. That's good. What do you think?"

She was so close to him, little puffs of her breath fanned his face and fogged up his glasses. Her volatile energy seemed to make the room quake. Nervously, he removed his glasses and tried to step back from her, only to find he was already up against the table. "I don't . . . know what to think," he confessed.

She shrugged. "I'll let it simmer for a while."

Taylor nodded inanely as Ali continued her scrutiny of him.

"I notice you've kept out of the press for the most part, through all the weddings. Hardly a photo or a quote from you, Taylor, although I'll bet the paparazzi have given it their best shot."

He cleared his throat. "I tend to keep a . . . low profile."

She grinned, her hand springing up to his chin, forcing his head sideways. "Not a bad profile at that, Taylor."

He swallowed hard as she relinquished her remarkably firm grip on him. "Look, Miss—"

"Ali. You'll be Taylor, I'll be Ali. I don't believe in wasting anything, words included. So why bother with Mr. This and Ms. That. Extra words, extra time. Anyway, Taylor, the point is you've got to know when to avoid publicity, and when to seek it. I don't mean you meaning *you*. I mean you meaning *me*. That's what I'm paid for. To know when to seek it, how to get it, how to play it for all it's worth. I'm good at that, Taylor. You put yourself in my hands and leave everything to me."

"Yes . . . Well . . ." He wiped at a bead of sweat that was running down the side of his neck.

She grinned, backing up a few steps—much to Taylor's relief. "I know. I come on too strong. It's another one of my bad habits. I'm always telling myself, 'Ali, take it slow at first.

Don't go in like a steamroller and flatten your client right out before he even gets a chance to take a breath.'" She raised both her hands in surrender. "Okay, Taylor. Shoot."

He blinked several times, then for want of something to do he stuck his glasses back on. "Excuse me?"

She dropped her hands to her hips. "You know. Fire away. Ask me questions."

Taylor was at a complete loss. This dynamo of a woman seemed to have a capacity to literally steal the breath from him. "Questions? Well, I really don't . . . Are you always like this?"

She grinned. "I'm calmer when I sleep. But not completely calm. I'm the sort that steals the blankets, grabs the extra pillows. And I kick sometimes." Her eyes sparkled. "But I don't snore."

"Who do you kick?" Taylor asked.

"You don't beat around the bush, do you, Taylor?"

He flushed. "Sorry. I guess that's none of my business. Sometimes I just sort of blurt things out." He smiled disarmingly. "A bad habit of mine."

She smiled back, thinking to herself, he didn't look half bad full-face, either. "No one of late."

Taylor didn't follow.

"I haven't slept with anyone of late." Her smile deepened. "Unless you want to count Bartholemew."

"Bartholemew?"

"My cat. Pesky critter. No matter how many times I kick him off the bed or grab his pillow out from under him, he hops right back on for more of the same treatment. Go figure."

Somehow Taylor could figure.

"You sleep with anyone, Taylor?" There was a deliberate pause, her smile inveigling. "I mean like a cat? Or maybe a dog? You don't cuddle up with Homer here, now, do you?"

"Hardly."

She moved toward him again. Taylor felt his muscles constrict and he experienced a strong desire to bolt, but realized he must already look foolish enough to this worldly PR maven.

As it turned out, she scooted right past him for a closer examination of Homer. "I've seen better-looking toasters," she quipped.

"Homer does a lot more than any toaster you've ever met." He could hear the ring of defensiveness in his tone.

So could Ali. "Actually, I haven't met that many toasters. My mom gave me one when I got my first apartment after college. But I always seemed to burn the bread. And one day I got fed up and tossed it out the window." The edges of her lips turned up, just perceptibly. "Don't worry. It was a basement apartment, so no one got clobbered."

"And since then?" he asked for want of something to say in response.

She winked at him. "I moved to an apartment on the fourteenth floor, so I figured I'd better give up toasters."

Taylor couldn't tell if she was pulling his leg. "Toaster ovens are a lot more reliable than the old-fashioned pop-up toasters."

"I guess you have a way with gadgets."

"A few times over the past couple of years I've been tempted to toss Homer out the window," Taylor confessed.

"I guess we both have low frustration levels," Ali said.

"I'm glad I didn't. Toss Homer out. He's really quite remarkable."

But Ali was only half listening, her eyes staring off into space. "Yes, quite remarkable."

"I really do believe Homer will practically sell himself," Taylor said, disconcerted by the fact she wasn't really paying attention.

Suddenly she swirled around to face him. "It *is* a great idea. The Fortune Man." She started circling him, giving him a most thorough inspection. "I told you it just needed to simmer a little. It's a great angle. Why, Taylor, I'm going to make you a household name. The Fortune Man with the fortune. The Fortune Man who won the tontine by staying single. The Fortune Man who chose fortune over love. Taylor, Taylor, can't you just see how this can work for us?"

"No," he said sharply. "No, you don't understand. I don't want to promote myself. I want to promote Homer."

"I know that, Taylor. But here's the gimmick. We market the invention with the man that invented it. And what a man. The Fortune Man. Why, I'll make you and your toy household words."

"Toy? Toy?" he sputtered. "Homer is no toy, Miss Spencer. For your edification, Homer happens to be—"

"Relax, Taylor. Relax." She started pacing, the wheels clicking like mad in her head. "Says what's on his mind, low frustration level and sensitive. I'll have to keep all that straight." She spun around again to face him. "What else, Taylor?"

"Look, Miss Spencer, I don't think this is—"

"Happens every time," she said philosophically.

Taylor squinted. "What happens?"

"First it's Miss Spencer, then it's Ali, and then invariably, as soon as I start pushing a little, we're back to Miss Spencer again. But don't worry, Taylor. That, too, will pass."

"You mean all of your clients have this...reaction to you?"

Ali laughed. "Yes. But most of them aren't as transparent about it as you are."

Taylor's mouth twitched. "I see."

"Don't be embarrassed, Taylor. I find it very endearing." She moved closer to him. "You have a lot of winning qualities."

"I do?"

"Of course, we'll have to do a bit of work on the rough edges. You've got brains, obviously, and a sense of humor when you let yourself relax a little. And the looks are good, Taylor. Not too showy, a touch on the aesthetic side, but then you're a scientist. Yes, the image can work for us, but we'll have to beef it up a little. A little more savoir faire so that every woman will want you in her bed—"

"Really, Miss Spencer," Taylor said, shocked.

"Oops, did I say bed? I meant kitchen," Ali corrected hurriedly, her cheeks coloring. "Every woman will want you in her kitchen."

"I don't want to be in any woman's kitchen."

"You won't be. They'll want you, but they can't have you. That's the angle. So, they'll have to settle for Homer. He'll be the closest to you they'll be able to get. My job is to make them happy to settle for second best."

"I really don't think—"

"Good. Leave the thinking to me, Taylor. Believe me, the image is the thing. I've been in the business long enough to know it isn't the product that sells, it's the image. And once we've got the right image for you, just having your name attached to something—even a stick of gum—will sell it." Her eyes lit up. "Hey, why not? Fortune gum. A great idea."

"I am not interested in gum. I'm interested in labor-saving inventions. I'm interested in products like Homer that will take the Fortune's store customer into the twenty-first century."

"That's great, Taylor. But you've got to enter the twenty-first century along with Homer."

"Really, Ali . . ."

She smiled. "That's better."

"What's better? Oh," he said, realizing he'd inadvertently gone back to calling her by her first name.

To give her her due, she didn't rub it in. Instead, she hopped onto the table at Homer's feet, swinging her long, shapely legs as she pulled a small notepad from her purse.

"Okay. Let's get down to the basics," she said, turning to a fresh page. "What do you do when you aren't tinkering?"

Taylor, whose gaze was fixed on the rhythmic swing of her legs, looked up, embarrassed. "What do I do?"

"For fun, Taylor. You do have fun, don't you?"

"Fun?"

"Taylor, come on. Give me something to work with here."

"Wait a minute. I haven't even decided whether . . . What I mean is, I'm not convinced your approach . . . I don't think this angle is . . . I'm not all that interesting as an . . . image."

Ali gave him a saucy smile. "It's my job to make you interesting. I just want to know what I have to work with. So how about it, Taylor? You can't tinker day and night." She arched a brow. "Can you?"

He hesitated. "Sometimes I play the bagpipes."

"The bagpipes?"

Taylor blinked several times. "It's a Scottish instrument—"

She grinned. "You caught me by surprise. But I can picture you on the bagpipes." She leaned forward a little, her gaze traveling brazenly down his body. "Do you wear a kilt?"

"I do own a kilt. But I don't wear it much. Knobby knees."

She continued smiling as she scribbled on her pad. "Okay," she said after a few moments. "What's your preference? Fair? Dark? Plump? On the lean side?"

"What are you talking about?"

"Women, Taylor. The opposite sex. You have heard of them?"

"I don't see what women have to do with any of this. Or the bagpipes. Look, Ali, I'm not one to rush into things. I need to let things . . . simmer, too." He was about to lie and say that he had another appointment. But lying had never come easily to Taylor so he settled for the truth.

"You overwhelm me, Ali. I've never come across a woman like you before. You make my head spin."

Ali slipped down off the desk. "Maybe that's not such a bad thing."

"Maybe . . . not. But I need some time to decide whether I can handle all . . . this." He was surprised to see a flicker of vulnerability in her eyes. "It isn't that I don't think you're good, Ali. I'm sure you are tops in your field. It's me. I just don't see myself as The Fortune Man. I'm sorry."

Ali silently chastised herself for coming on so strong. She was blowing it. The PR job of a lifetime, the chance to finally make a big enough name for herself in the business to open her own place—and she was blowing it. Okay, she told herself, the least she could do was bow out gracefully. "Maybe you're right, Taylor," she said with a sigh. "Maybe we aren't the right mix." She held out her hand. This time Taylor took hold immediately. "I'm sorry, Taylor. It could have been fun."

Now that he'd been quick enough to grab her hand, strangely enough he was unwilling to let it go. "Yes. I'm sorry, too, Ali."

"Well, I guess that's it, then." She glanced down at her hand still in his. Taylor looked, too. Reluctantly he released it.

She slid her freed hand into her purse and brought out a business card. "Just in case, after you let things simmer, you decide to give it a whirl." She gave Homer a quick glance. "You and your friend."

He took the card and read it. By the time he looked up, she was gone, leaving as quickly as she'd arrived.

"Hey," he said, "you never even got to see Homer in action. . . ."

2

ALI SPENCER PUSHED the chicken à la king around her plate with her fork, but it just seemed like too much of an effort to get a forkful to her mouth. Finally she let the fork go altogether.

Ali's roommate, Sara Brooks, a petite, dark-haired woman in her mid-twenties, gave her friend a rueful look. "Hey, stop being so down, kiddo. He could change his mind and give you a call. He took your card, didn't he?"

Ali's brown eyes, usually sparkling with mischief, had a dull, listless glaze as she looked across at Sara. "It's all my own fault. I was too damn pushy, too self-assured, too overwhelming. The last was his word."

"He actually told you straight out that you 'overwhelmed' him?"

Ali nodded. "I went about it all wrong. I should have played it soft, gentle. I should have been low-key."

Sara laughed. "That I'd like to see."

"I wish his grandmother had given me more warning. All she told me was that he was reserved." She smiled wryly. "Jessica's great at understatement. But I should have seen the writing on the wall. I knew that he'd kept out of the spotlight through all his brothers' marriages. I could have figured that meant more than that he was just camera shy. The guy's turned shyness into an art form."

She rose from the table and began pacing. Bartholemew, Ali's overfed tabby, was quick to take her place, lapping up her chicken à la king with gusto. Neither woman paid the cat any mind.

"And even if I didn't have a clue before I walked into his office—or more accurately, barged in like a fireman—one look at the guy and I should have known he wasn't exactly Mr. Smoothie," Ali went on, self-effacingly. "But I was too busy making my pitch: I just grabbed hold of him and pushed him into the deep end of the pool only to find out the dumb cluck couldn't swim to save himself."

"What was he like?" Sara asked. She, like thousands of other single young women, had followed the romantic exploits of the other three Fortune brothers in the media, and like those other woman, had spun more than a few romantic fantasies in the process. She was very curious about the last remaining Fortune bachelor.

Ali sighed. "He's not really a dumb cluck. He's probably quite brilliant. More like the bashful-professor type. You know, painfully self-conscious, devoid of sophistication. And my guess is he's not exactly the most experienced of men when it comes to either women or business. He's the kind of guy that if he told me he still believed in Santa Claus, I wouldn't be surprised."

Sara laughed. "He sounds awfully simple."

Ali turned to her roommate. "I think he is simple. I don't mean simpleminded, though. Like I said, he's the brainy type. What I mean is, he isn't complicated. And he's not your typical game-player. There doesn't seem to be any subterfuge, any hidden agendas at work. I think he's basically honest, decent and straightforward." She sat back down in her chair, vacated by Bartholemew now that he'd licked her plate clean. Ali merely pushed the empty plate out of the way and propped her elbows on the table. "He was really quite refreshing."

"Don't tell me he got to you, kiddo? Ali Spencer, the gal who keeps her heart in a steel vault."

"Oh, please, Sara. Don't get carried away. I merely said that I found him refreshing after the typical slick, superficial, backstabbing operators I usually tangle with," Ali was quick to counter. Then she shrugged. "Not that I could market him that way. He'd need a thorough overhaul. He could use a little more muscle and a lot more self-confidence. Plus, he looks like he buys his clothes at church rummage sales. And his hair—I'll bet dollars to donuts he hacks it off himself with dull-bladed scissors. A snip here, a snip there, everywhere a snip, snip...."

Both woman laughed. But then Ali turned wistful.

"My plan was to turn Taylor into The Fortune Man."

"The Fortune Man?"

"That was my pitch. I'd clean him up, give him some spit and polish, have him seen in all the right places, create an air of mystery and allure about him, and in no time flat I'd have every woman from the West Coast to the East Coast drooling over The Fortune Man, the last single brother of the lot, the survivor who claimed the tontine, making him the sole owner of the Fortune empire and one of the wealthiest and most sought-after bachelors in the West." Ali rose again, scooping Bartholemew up into her arms. "Will The Fortune Man, too, give up all that wealth, power and freedom, for love? That's the question that would be on the mind of every red-blooded American woman in the country if I had free rein. And they'd all be fantasizing about being the woman who could make him give it all up. They'd dream about him, think about him, read every piece of copy about him they could get their hands on. And once that happens, he'd be able to sell them anything. The Brooklyn Bridge. Hell, even Homer."

"Who's Homer?"

"Not *who*. *What*. Homer, the robot."

"You mean . . . like R2D2 from *Star Wars*?" Sara asked.

Ali nodded. "I even told him I'd seen better-looking toasters. Me and my big mouth." She shook her head. "Really, Homer was kind of cute. Lots of dials and switches and colorful knobs. Not that I couldn't have come up with a few alterations to give Homer a classier appearance." She propped her chin on her knuckles and sighed. "I never even gave Taylor a chance to show me how Homer worked."

TAYLOR FORTUNE HAD trouble concentrating on work for the rest of the day. Even Homer lay abandoned on the worktable, the new adjustment to his rotary arm still untested. At close to six, Taylor's secretary, Rhonda, popped her head in.

"I'll be leaving now, Mr. Fortune, unless you want me to work late. . . ."

Taylor looked up from the business card he'd been staring at. "Oh, no, Rhonda. Thanks. I won't be staying much longer myself."

Rhonda knew that he rarely left the building before ten most nights, using all his free time to tinker with his robot and the other gadgets he was always working on.

"I could have the deli send up a couple of sandwiches. . . ."

"Oh, no. That's okay. I'm not really hungry."

"Well, there's an apple in my top drawer if you want a snack. And the number of the deli's in my Rolodex file," Rhonda said, before slipping out.

At about seven-thirty, Taylor was still sitting at his desk, trying to analyze an annual report but making no headway at all. He looked over at Homer. Slowly, a smile came to Taylor's lips. "Better-looking toasters . . ."

He picked up the business card again, running his index finger lightly over the embossed name—Ali Spencer. In the upper right-hand corner was her work number; in the upper left, her home number. He stared at her home number for several minutes, then resolutely set the card down.

"No," he mumbled to himself. "It's crazy. She doesn't get it. You're the one that's supposed to get the publicity, not me. Publicity's the last thing I want." He stopped, then stared at Homer. "Look at me. I'm talking out loud to you now. I've got her to thank for that."

He rose and walked over to the robot, turning a switch at the side of its head. Lights flashed on, and the earlier groans and high-pitched whines were replaced by a nice, soothing hum as Homer came to life. With the flick of another switch, soft mood music replaced the pleasant hum. A nice touch, he thought. "Okay, Homer. Let's test that arm of yours out now."

Just as he was about to run the robot through its paces, wrench in hand for any additional adjustments, his phone rang. Startled, Taylor dropped the wrench on his foot. Cursing and hobbling, he crossed the room and snatched up the receiver.

"Yes?" he snapped.

"Taylor?"

Ali Spencer's distinctive raspy voice had made an indelible impression on Taylor, and as soon as he heard his name spoken, he knew it was her. He felt an immediate rush of nerves. And anticipation.

"Yes." This *yes* was spoken in a much softer tone.

"I hope I'm not disturbing you."

There was a long pause while Taylor switched the receiver from one hand to the other, wiping his sweaty palm on his pants. "No."

"Listen . . ."

"I've been thinking about you."

Ali was taken aback. "You have?"

"Yes." There was another pause. "I haven't been able to do much of anything else since you left," he confessed.

"You haven't?"

"I don't like your plan, Ali."

"I realized that this morning. That's why I called. You see, I was thinking about you, too."

Taylor switched the receiver again. "You were?"

"And . . . Homer."

"You were thinking about Homer, too?"

"I realized I never did get to see Homer in action. I guess I was so caught up in—"

"Would you like to?"

"What?"

"Would you like to see Homer in action?"

"Why . . . yes. Yes, very much. I think that would be—"

"When?"

"Well . . . anytime. Anytime at all. I mean, anytime that would be convenient for—"

"How about now?"

"Now? You mean *right now?*"

"As soon as you get here. I could send my driver for you."

"Oh, that won't be necessary. I can drive—"

"I can't."

"You can't drive?"

"No."

"Why not?"

"I never learned. I never went many places. And I've always had a driver and car at my disposal."

"Oh."

"But I could learn."

Ali laughed. "Driving's no big deal. If I always had a driver and car at my disposal—"

"I'll send him over, then."

"No, I didn't mean . . . Well, sure. Okay. Why not? I don't get to wallow in luxury every day."

"Good. So, I'll see you soon."

"Even sooner if your driver speeds," she said with a laugh.

When Taylor placed the receiver in the cradle, he noticed that his hand was trembling. He pressed the intercom button that connected with the garage. "Daniel, I need you to pick up a Miss Ali Spencer and bring her back here."

If Daniel was surprised by his employer's request, it in no way showed in his voice. "Yes, sir. Where does she live?"

Taylor frowned. Where did she live? He looked at Ali's business card but the only address was her place of work. "I—uh—I'll call you right back, Daniel."

Feeling like a complete fool, he quickly dialed Ali's number.

Her line was busy. *Damn.*

A moment before he tried her number again, his phone rang. He grabbed up the receiver. "Hello?"

"I'm at 34 River Drive, apartment 14C."

THE WAIT SEEMED LIKE an eternity, but then there she was—Ali, who appeared so worldly and confident, her wild copper curls bobbing every which way as she strode into the room. Her enticing red suit and black pumps had been replaced by jeans and an oversize sweatshirt, but oddly enough Taylor found her appearance now even more bedazzling. He watched her as she crossed the room, shoulders back, jaw jutting forward with just a perceptible hint of defiance. As she drew closer, he saw that she had a few freckles scattered across the bridge of her nose. And then he noticed a faint scar just over her left eyebrow. He liked the imperfections. They gave her a touch of vulnerability, a feeling he was exceedingly well acquainted with.

Ali was quite aware that her arrival had raised Taylor's temperature. She saw the boyishly hungry way he was taking her in. There was no question in her mind that he found her attractive. The question was, should she use it on him, play up to him to win him over?

She didn't consider the question for very long, chastising herself for even raising it. Sure, she'd come here to win Taylor over. She wanted the account. She wanted it badly. And it wasn't that she hadn't used her feminine wiles when necessary in the past if it came down to wooing an account. But that had been with clients who knew how the game was played. A little flirtation that never got off the ground was sometimes part of the process. Ali was an ace at the game. But she couldn't play the game with Taylor. He was just too susceptible. She had a strong hunch he wouldn't know what to make of it, how to handle it. He'd probably get the wrong idea.

Taylor didn't know what to say. His heart was racing. He had the feeling of being on a runaway train. Oddly enough, the sensation was more exhilarating than terrifying. "How was the drive?" he asked finally.

She grinned. "Great. I had a few drinks, watched *The Honeymooners* on the TV built into the bar, made a few long-distance calls.... Hey, I'm joking."

"It would have been okay," he hurriedly reassured her, smiling self-consciously. "I don't watch much TV. I don't drink all that much, either. Oh, would you like a drink? Or something to eat? Or both? You could have both. Something to eat and something to drink."

"I made a real ass of myself this morning, Taylor. Sorry. I just had to get that off my chest. Sure, I'd love something to eat. And drink."

"No, you didn't. I was just . . . caught off guard. I don't know. Maybe you were . . . right. I mean . . . that I need to enter the twenty-first century along with Homer."

"No. Why should you? You've got every right to live your life the way you choose. And you're *fortunate* enough," she added with a smile, "to have the choice."

"I do tend to be . . . pretty reclusive." He didn't know what to do with his hands so he stuck them in his trouser pockets. "I mean, that was okay when I wasn't . . . president. I never really expected this to happen. I never really expected any of my brothers to marry. I don't really understand how it happened to them." But somewhere in the back of his mind he was beginning to get an inkling.

"I guess being president must be tough for a guy who doesn't like the limelight."

"Oh, don't get me wrong. There's plenty about being president that I like. Take Homer, here. Or some of the other timesaving household inventions I'm working on. If one of my brothers were still running the show I wouldn't have gotten much support for marketing them, making them a focal point of Fortune's."

"Don't they believe in your . . . inventions?"

Taylor grinned. "Some of my gadgets have backfired. But, hell—excuse me—heck, all inventors have their down times." He frowned. "Say, I don't usually talk so much. And here I almost forgot you wanted something to eat and drink. What'll it be? Deli sandwich and beer? Steak and wine? Caviar and champagne?"

Ali laughed. "First a chauffeur-driven limo, then caviar and champagne? Taylor, Taylor, you're making my head spin now."

He beamed. "Caviar and champagne, it is."

Before she could tell him she wasn't serious, he grabbed her hand and led her out the door. "Where are we going?"

"To the gourmet-food department, of course. Where else would we find caviar?"

"TAYLOR FORTUNE, THIS is positively decadent. Do you know that I have never eaten beluga caviar before in my entire life?" She leaned forward on the sofa in what looked for all the world like an elegant penthouse living room but was actually a display room in the Fortune's furniture department. "Here," she said, clasping the neck of the half-full champagne bottle and pulling it out of the silver bucket filled with ice. "Have another glass?" An empty bottle lay on the mauve carpeted floor. Beside Taylor.

Taylor had lost count of how many glasses he's already had, but he vaguely remembered he'd stopped protesting after the fourth glass or so. As Ali filled his goblet, some of the champagne spilled over the rim. It was difficult to tell whose hand was unsteadier, hers or his.

He took a long swallow, then stretched back out on the carpet.

"Are you okay?" Ali asked.

"Never better," he mumbled.

She'd had about three glasses of champagne herself, which was over her limit. But somehow she was feeling particularly festive and fanciful, stretched out on this six-thousand-dollar butter-soft cream leather sofa, feasting on Dom Pérignon champagne and beluga caviar. She set the bottle back in the ice bucket, then dipped her fingertips wantonly into the crystal dish filled with the caviar and slid them, one at a time, into her mouth.

Taylor watched her, mesmerized.

Her gaze met his. "Are you sure you don't want any caviar?" she asked, extending a sample on her finger for him to taste.

Taylor had never cared for caviar, but then he'd never before had such a seductive offering. He rose slightly, propping himself on his elbows, parting his lips. Ali slipped her finger into his mouth.

Too late, she realized it wasn't such a smart move. No sooner had his lips closed around her finger than she felt such an intense rush of desire that she nearly rolled right off the couch and on top of him. Only her even more intense desire for self-preservation stopped her. She plucked her finger out of his mouth so quickly her nail snagged his lip. A pinprick of blood oozed out.

Ali gasped. "Oh, Taylor, I've made you bleed."

He grinned tipsily. "I don't feel a thing."

She leaned closer to examine the severity of the damage. Taylor rose on his elbows again to help her. She looked from his bruised lip to his warm hazel eyes. He was staring at her, his breathing shallow.

He smiled crookedly. "I think I may be a bit…drunk, Ali."

She smiled back, her gaze still fixed on his. "I think you may be right, Taylor."

"I have this incredibly strong urge to kiss you, Ali."

"Now, Taylor…that's probably an urge you shouldn't give in to."

"Yes. You're probably right." He dropped back down onto the carpet.

Ali was shaken by the intensity of her disappointment. *It must be the champagne,* she told herself. She swung her legs to the floor and sat up. "I've got to go home, Taylor. And so do you."

He made no response and his eyes were closed. She leaned down to shake his shoulder, thinking he might have passed out. "Taylor?"

His eyes sprang open. "Ali?"

For some reason she didn't want to consider, her heart was beating wildly. She was probably going to regret this in the morning. And so would Taylor. Then again, he'd had so much champagne he mightn't even remember anything in the morning.

She leaned lower. He rose. Somewhere midmotion their lips collided. It was a clumsy meeting but they both made the most of it.

THE ROOM WAS SPINNING. Taylor groaned and closed his eyes, only to discover they were already closed. He made a vague attempt at opening them, but that made everything spin more.

"Here, drink this," a familiar voice ordered.

He squinted up at his grandmother. There were two of her. They were both holding out a glass of putrid brown liquid for him to drink.

"Go on. Don't be a baby about it," she said.

"What is it?" he asked hoarsely, feeling a decidedly unpleasant taste creeping up the back of his throat.

"It's an old recipe for curing what ails you. It's called a prairie oyster. Don't ask me what's in it. Just drink it."

He lifted his hand somewhere between the two glasses he was seeing and Jessica clasped his wrist, depositing the glass in his hand. He made a face as he swallowed the drink down, but a couple of minutes later he did feel a bit better.

"What happened?" he asked dazedly.

"Don't you remember?"

He tried to think. "My head feels kind of foggy."

"You don't remember getting together with Ali Spencer at the store last night?"

Jessica's question slowly sank in. Forgetting about his pounding head, Taylor popped up in bed. "I remember . . . some of it. The caviar . . . and the champagne." He smiled sheepishly. "A lot of champagne." Quickly his smile winked out. "I remember...kissing her, and then..." He didn't know what had happened then. He couldn't remember anything after that kiss. "I don't know what came over me," he admitted. How carried away had he gotten?

Taylor grabbed for the phone on his bedside table. "I'd better call her. I should apologize. I had too much champagne. Not that that's any excuse."

Jessica fought back a smile. Even in her wildest fantasies she hadn't expected things to progress so quickly.

"What did I do with her phone number? Oh, it's on her business card." He frowned, trying to remember what he'd done with it. "My trousers. I put it in one of the pockets in my trousers."

"I'm afraid you're out of luck, then."

"The card's gone?"

"No, dear. Your trousers are gone. According to Daniel, you came home last night without them."

Taylor's complexion went from red to white. "I came home . . . without my pants?"

"Yes, dear," Jessica said nonchalantly, picking up the empty glass. "Well, unless you'd like me to fix you another prairie oyster, I've got a garden-club luncheon to attend."

Taylor numbly shook his head.

"I'm sure she's listed in the phone book," Jessica said before she exited.

After his grandmother left, he just lay in bed imagining one embarrassing scenario after another. He was too embarrassed, now, to call Ali. What would he say? How could he apologize when he didn't even know what he was apologizing for? The ring of the phone jolted him out of his worrisome reverie.

"Hi, Taylor. How are you feeling?"

"Ali?"

"I called at the store but they said you hadn't come in. Not that I was surprised. Pretty rotten hangover, huh?"

"Listen, Ali, I don't know what to say. I'm so embarrassed by—"

"Come on, Taylor. You let your hair down and had some fun. I had fun, too."

"You did?"

"I loved it. It was positively decadent. Not that I could take a steady diet of that sort of thing. I can only be wanton like that just so often."

"Oh, God," he moaned.

"Taylor? Are you okay?"

"You aren't...upset? You don't feel...things got too...out of hand?"

"Come on, Taylor. It's nothing to make a fuss over. We had some champagne, I devoured a whole jar of beluga caviar, we kissed—"

"And...then?"

"You don't remember?"

Taylor shut his eyes. "No," he said weakly.

There was a silence that to Taylor seemed interminable. Then he heard Ali's soft laugh. "Oh, Taylor, nothing else happened. It was just one little ole kiss, and then...you kind of dozed off. I phoned down to Daniel and he heaved you up over his shoulder, dropped me off at my place and took you home. You have nothing to worry about, Taylor. Your virtue is intact."

"Then what happened to my trousers?" It was hard getting the sentence out.

"Your...what?"

"I came home without my trousers. I thought...when you said... Well, you used the words *decadent* and... *wanton*."

Ali laughed again. "I was talking about the beluga. And the Dom Pérignon champagne. Really, Taylor, what kind of girl do you think I am?" she teased.

Taylor muttered an apology and hung up. He had never felt so humiliated. Later that afternoon, he learned from Daniel what had happened to his trousers. It seemed that he'd insisted on taking a half-full bottle of champagne into the limo. After dropping Ali off, Taylor had gone to pour himself another glass of the bubbly, only to spill it all over his trousers. With drunken aplomb, he'd removed his sodden trousers and blithely tossed them out the window, mumbling something about them not being suitable attire for The Fortune Man....

3

BOTH ALI AND HER roommate, Sara, were fast asleep when the doorbell rang at seven-fifteen on Saturday morning. Ali, the deeper sleeper of the two, didn't hear a thing. Sara tried her best to ignore the ring, even stuffing her pillow over her head, but whoever was at the door was persistent. Groggily, she tossed off the covers, threw on her bathrobe and shuffled to the front door. She was in the middle of a yawn as she opened the door.

Her mouth stayed open.

"Good morning. My name is Homer. I am your all-purpose helper. Today is Saturday, June 22nd. I hope you had a very good sleep. The weather is bright and sunny. I will be happy to begin my chores now."

Sara tripped over her feet backing away from the door as the three-foot-high gleaming metal visitor waddled robot-fashion into the house. Slowly, Sara's mouth changed from an O to a wily smile.

"Uh…this way, Homer," Sara said, hurrying ahead of the robot and guiding him toward Ali's room. After a quick knock, Sara opened her roommate's door. "Hey, Ali, you've got company."

"Go away," Ali muttered sleepily.

Sara winked at Homer as he marched into the room. "Don't mind her. She's always crabby in the morning." Laughing, Sara exited, closing the bedroom door behind her.

Ali went to pull the cover up over her head so she could go back to sleep. But the cover wouldn't budge. She tugged harder, only to have the cover snatched right out of her hand.

"What the . . . ?" Irritated and confused, she rolled over, squinting her eyes open.

And then Ali saw who—or rather what—was playing tug-of-war with her. Startled, she let out a scream. Her voice activated the robot.

"Good morning. My name is Homer. I am your all-purpose helper. Today is Saturday, June 22nd. I hope you had a very good sleep. The weather is bright and sunny. I will be happy to begin my chores now."

Ali sat there in bed, staring dumbfounded at the robot as it proceeded to take the cover from her bed, then began removing the fitted bottom sheet. When Homer got to the five-foot-seven-inch obstruction in the middle of the bed, he straightened and looked right at her. It seemed for all the world like he could actually see her. It was downright eerie.

Ali rubbed her eyes. Maybe this was all a crazy dream.

AFTER SARA DEPOSITED Homer in Ali's room, she returned to the front door of the apartment, opening it. Standing out in the hall, as she'd expected, was Taylor Fortune. He managed an awkward smile.

"I thought . . . Ali . . . Miss Spencer . . . lived alone."

Sara introduced herself, wishing she'd thought to brush her teeth, fix her hair and put on a little makeup before her first meeting with "The Fortune Man."

"Do you want to come inside?" Sara was asking when they both heard the shrill scream coming from behind Ali's closed door.

Sara and Taylor looked at each other, then both made a beeline for Ali's bedroom. Sara threw open her door and then burst into laughter.

"This isn't funny," Ali snapped, flailing her arms and legs in midair as the powerful little robot held her in its firm grasp several inches above the mattress. Then Ali saw Taylor. She glared at him. "Tell this monster to put me down this instant," she demanded.

"Good morning. My name is Homer. . . ."

Taylor rushed over, but he was so upset he pushed the wrong button. Instead of Homer's arms straightening so that Ali could free herself, the robot's voice box shut off and cheery polka music came out of the speaker in its forehead.

"Taylor," Ali warned, "if this—this thing—doesn't release me, I'm going to take a jackhammer to it."

"Please, Ali, just . . . stay calm," Taylor pleaded as he pressed what should have been the right button. Only it didn't work. Homer's arms didn't budge. Another "minor" kink.

Sara was still giggling. "Kind of reminds me of King Kong and Faye Wray. Only I guess Kong was a little taller. And hairier." Sara began laughing in earnest again.

Taylor anxiously pressed another button. Homer stepped back, carrying a kicking, screaming, nightie-clad Ali in his arms. Polka music still emanated from his speaker. "Shut him off, damn it. I mean it, Taylor."

Taylor pressed the deactivator button. Homer came to a dead stop, the music cut off mid-note. The problem was, the robot simply froze in place, his arms still bent upward, holding Ali in his viselike grip.

"I don't know what could have gone wrong," Taylor said. "This never happened before."

Ali was steaming. She also felt utterly ridiculous, caught in the clutches of the mechanical monster. And it didn't help that Sara was laughing her head off. "Get out of here!" she shouted. As she saw Taylor turn to leave, she snapped, "Not you. Her!"

Sara tried to stop laughing and look contrite. She didn't succeed at either and figured this was as good a time as any to make her exit. "Could I bring you coffee?" she managed between giggles. "You're always a bear before you have your morning coffee, Ali."

"Bring a hacksaw," Ali hissed, trying to tug her very short, not to mention very sheer, nightie down over her thighs. But the material was caught up in Homer's mechanical arms and she only succeeded in tearing the hem. "Perfect," she muttered acidly. "This is just perfect."

Taylor was busy trying not to notice Ali's state of undress as he fumbled with Homer's inner workings. When he heard her gown rip, though, he glanced up at her. "I really am sorry about this, Ali. I'll . . . pay for the . . ." He didn't finish the sentence, his embarrassment getting the best of him.

For some reason Ali couldn't fathom, she felt sorry for Taylor. "I guess someday I'll laugh about this."

Taylor's eyes met hers. "You will?"

She smiled crookedly. "I must look pretty damn silly."

"No. You look . . . beautiful."

Ali was used to compliments, but Taylor's managed to bring a flush to her cheeks. No woman looked her best first thing in the morning—especially when she was in a ripped nightie, clutched in the arms of a mechanical monster. But Ali knew Taylor wasn't just handing her a line. For whatever it was worth, he meant it. Sincerity. One of Taylor's shining traits. And one that threw her.

She tried to make light of the whole ludicrous, embarrassing situation. "I've heard of unique seductions before, Taylor, but this one takes the cake."

"Oh, it wasn't—I didn't—I was just trying to impress you with . . . Homer's capabilities."

Ali grinned. "I'm impressed. A little more impressed than I care to be."

"I'm really sorry about this, Ali."

"You said that already. Just do something, Taylor."

"Yes, yes, I will. Just give me a couple of minutes and I'll . . . have you freed." He left off his fidgeting with Homer's insides to grab the cover from the floor and throw it over Ali.

For it all she was touched. "One little steel monster and one knight in shining armor. Quite a combo, Taylor."

"I should have realized . . . you'd still be in bed," Taylor muttered as he knelt behind the robot, checking out its operating system.

"It would have been a good guess. It isn't even seven-thirty."

"I just wanted to be sure I got you in. And I guess I'm so used to getting up at the crack of dawn that I just sort of figure everyone else is up, too."

"How are we doing back there?" she asked, craning her neck back to see how he was progressing.

"I think it's just a loose wire. It just needs a little . . . There, that should do it."

Taylor got to his feet and came around to face both Ali and Homer. Their eyes met and held. Taylor's and Ali's, that is. Homer's black-button eyes had a faraway look, although his smiley mouth definitely gave the impression the mechanical robot gone amok was enjoying himself.

"I wouldn't blame you," Taylor said gently, "if you tossed both of us out on our ears and never had another thing to do with us."

"I'm in no position to do any tossing at the moment, Taylor," she said with a faint smile.

"This was a dumb idea." And another seriously dumb idea was taking hold of him as he stood there staring at Ali ensnared in the arms of his robot. He fought the idea and the urge, as he flicked the activator switch.

"Good morning. My name is Homer. . . ."

Then Taylor pressed a button. Without warning, Homer's arms shot out so abruptly that Ali literally flew into Taylor, catching them both completely by surprise. The next thing they knew they were on the floor, tangled up in the cover and in each other's arms. Homer dismissed the pair with a 180-degree revolution, blithely returning to his bed-changing chore.

Ali and Taylor looked embarrassed, then astonished. And then they burst into laughter, falling against each other as they tried to help each other to their feet. Ali was laughing so hard, tears were running down her cheeks. She swiped at them, looking up into Taylor's laughing face. But then he stopped laughing. Something fluttered in his eyes, and his features turned tender, enigmatic, apologetic all at once.

"Oh, Taylor," she murmured. "What am I going to do about you?"

And then, again without warning, his lips were on hers. Ali felt like her whole world had gone topsy-turvy. Here was the awkward, tentative Mr. Fortune, kissing her with a sureness that took her completely by surprise.

Instinctively, her lips parted under his and she felt his tongue slip into her mouth. The cover swished to the floor as her arms wound around his neck. Even as she moved against him, she told herself she should stop this crazy nonsense, get a grip on herself, and tell Mr. Taylor Fortune with his oh-so-kissable lips to take his wily little monster and clear out. But it felt as if there were this giant invisible hand pressing against the small of her back, pushing her into his arms.

Her fingers wove through his shaggy hair as he wrapped his arms around her. A burning sensation zigzagged through her body, tingling through her limbs. She felt weak. It had been a long time since she'd felt this way, and not since she was a teen had a mere kiss provoked such arousal. Okay— one super whammy of a kiss. Not like that clumsy peck they'd shared in a state of intoxication the other night at the department store.

Taylor was giving his all to his kiss, exploring her mouth in his own good time. And Ali had no desire to rush him along. It was Homer who broke it up.

"I have removed the linens on the bed. Please furnish me with fresh linens so that I can complete my task...."

"GOOD COFFEE," TAYLOR commented as he sat at the kitchen table across from Ali and Sara.

Sara smiled. "Believe it or not, it's Fortune's's own brand. I'm a nut for their—I mean your—gourmet department. Everything from coffee beans to— Well, to nuts. Aren't I, Ali?"

Ali gave her a dry look. "Nuts? Definitely."

Sara chuckled. "Well," she said, rising and rubbing her hands together. "I guess I'll get my morning run in now. And then I'll probably stop at the gym for a while. Probably won't get back here for at least a couple of hours." She gave Ali a knowing smile.

Ali didn't smile back. She was feeling very uneasy—the aftereffects of Taylor's kiss.

A minute later Ali heard the front door shut. She emitted a long sigh.

"I'm so used to dealing with shrewd, glib, devious guys, Taylor. You've gone and thrown me for a loop."

"You don't look too happy about it. I probably shouldn't have kissed you again. I don't honestly remember our first kiss all that well." He hesitated, a beguiling smile lighting his face. "I won't forget this one, though."

Neither would Ali, but she was more reticent about admitting such things. When Ali's heart started to flutter, she usually beat a hasty retreat. And it had been a long time since it had fluttered like this. "You are impossible, Taylor," she murmured.

"Does that mean the deal's off?" he asked softly.

"What deal?"

"The Fortune Man."

Ali could only stare at him.

"I realize Homer wasn't on his best behavior, but I know I can iron out the kinks. I guess the question is, can you iron out the . . . kinks in me. Turning me into The Fortune Man is going to be no mean trick, Ali. That is, if you—"

"Taylor," Ali said, springing up from her chair, "nothing turns me on more than a tough challenge." Well, that wasn't altogether true. Taylor's kissing talents ran a close second. But now that she'd finally gotten his cooperation, she was going to have to get control of herself. And Taylor.

She pulled him to his feet. "When can you start?"

"Start? Start what?"

"We have to get you new clothes, do something about your hair. . . ."

"My hair?"

"I don't suppose you'd consider some blond highlights? Guys are doing it all the time. Or one gold streak. It would give you a definite rakish look."

"A gold steak?"

"No. No, forget it. That would be too blatant." She ran her fingers through his hair, this time with nothing on her mind but business. "Good texture. And the color's not bad. I'll bet the sun lightens it naturally in the summer."

"Not really. I'm not out in the sun all that much in the summer. Or in the winter."

"Don't you sail?"

Taylor shook his head.

"Golf?"

"No."

"Tennis?"

"I played a little as a kid, but I'm not very...athletic."

"Okay, we'll start with sailing. Sailors have a special rugged allure."

"I don't think sailing's such a good idea. Adam dragged me out on his sloop a couple of times and I—"

"Adam's got a sloop? Great. You think he'll let us borrow it?"

"Well...yes, I suppose. But I'm trying to tell you—"

"Don't worry, Taylor. I'm a pretty good skipper. You'll catch on in no time. The Fortune Man's got to sail."

Taylor had to smile. "You know him better than I do."

Ali grinned. "This is going to be great, Taylor. I'm going to put my heart and soul into this campaign."

Taylor smiled boyishly. "I can't ask for more than that."

Ali's grin faded. "We need some ground rules, though. I mean...now that we're actually working together," she said soberly. "This really has to be strictly...business, Taylor. I know I share a certain amount of responsibility for that...kiss, before. But I just don't think it would be smart.... We don't want things to get complicated, do we?"

"No. I don't suppose we do."

"So, we're in agreement, right?"

He took a moment before responding. "Right."

Ali stretched out her hand. "Let's shake on it."

Taylor took her hand in his. It took all his willpower not to pull her into his arms again. But Ali was right. The last thing in the world he wanted was to fall in love. That would be his undoing—as surely as it had been Adam's, Pete's and Tru's. Before he knew it, he, too, would be popping the question. And then it would be goodbye to Fortune's. If for no other reason than that his brothers would never forgive him for letting the company fall into outside hands, Taylor had to keep his head.

"WHAT DO YOU MEAN, he's hired her?" Peter said to Adam, leaning forward in his chair in the dining room of the country club. Tru looked incredulously at Adam.

"You heard me," Adam repeated. "He struck a deal with Ali Spencer."

"She's going to do the Homer promotion?" Peter asked.

"Homer? Oh, not just Homer. It seems our hotshot publicist has it in her head to promote our kid brother. According to Taylor, Ms. Spencer believes that by promoting him, he'll be able to sell the Fortune's consumer any product from robots to Fortune's gum."

"Fortune's *gum?*" Tru and Peter muttered at the same time.

"That isn't the half of it," Adam said dryly. "Let me tell you about the night he arrived home without his pants...."

THE THREE FORTUNE WIVES were having their own little pow-wow around a white-linen-covered table at Café Gaufre in downtown Denver. Eve Fortune, looking especially radiant in a pale pink maternity sundress, eyed her two sisters-in-law, Elizabeth and Sasha. Elizabeth was in town interviewing for a neuropsychiatric position at Denver General. Sasha had returned with Tru from Moscow to focus their attention for the next couple of months on the shop they were opening in Denver featuring Russian imports.

Eve pushed aside her Caesar salad. "We've got to do something to help the cause of true love, ladies. The word I got from Adam is that all of our husbands are bound and determined to put pressure on Taylor to cancel his PR deal with Ali Spencer because they're convinced he's already smitten with her," Eve said.

"Already smitten?" Elizabeth echoed. "But Pete says he's only seen her a couple of times...."

Sasha grinned. "How long did it take Pete or Adam or Tru to be smitten?" She posed the question in her thick Russian accent, then took a bite of her sole amandine.

Eve gave the other two knowing looks. "How long did it take any of us, for that matter?"

All three women laughed, then Eve got serious again. "So, are we all agreed that we have to do something?"

"But what can we do?" Elizabeth asked, buttering a piece of crusty French bread. "I don't suppose we can just sit around and hope that lightning strikes twice," she added with a broad smile. Her husband Pete's bout with a lightning bolt had been the trigger of their rollicking romantic affair.

"A good adventure would do the trick," Sasha mused, thinking about how the danger and excitement of tracking down smugglers had added fuel to the flames of passion between her and Tru.

Eve sighed. "I think the first thing we need is a reading of where Ali Spencer stands. Taylor may be smitten, but from everything I've heard about his public-relations wunderkind, she's not the type to go losing her heart over our bashful, unworldly, reclusive brother-in-law."

"Maybe he'll change. Love *can* change a man," Elizabeth pointed out, with a twinkle in her eye. "Especially a Fortune man."

Eve and Sasha agreed wholeheartedly.

"I know," Eve said enthusiastically. "Adam and I will host a little party. Just the family and a few friends."

"A fine idea," Sasha said. "But do you think Taylor will invite Ali?"

"He will if we're celebrating a birth," Eve replied conspiratorially.

Sasha and Elizabeth gave Eve a puzzled look. "But you aren't due for two months," Elizabeth pointed out. "Besides, why do you think he'd ask Ali?"

Eve grinned. "I'm talking about the birth of Homer. Taylor's little robot. The one Ali Spencer's been hired to promote."

Elizabeth and Sasha thought it a splendid idea and they began to make plans right then and there.

A few minutes later a waiter approached their table. "Will there be anything else, ladies? Perhaps I can interest you in some coffee or dessert?"

Eve eyed her coconspirators. Both women nodded. "Yes," Eve said to the waiter. "Definitely dessert. We're throwing caution to the wind today."

"No, no, no. That's all wrong," Ali muttered, tossing shirts, ties and trousers out of Taylor's closet.

"You discard much more and I'll be walking around in my birthday suit," Taylor teased.

But Ali wasn't paying attention. She was heading for his bureau. Taylor warded her off, pressing his hand against his top drawer as she started to pull it open.

She gave him an amused look. "Diary? Love letters? Top-secret drawings for a Homer clone?"

Taylor flushed. "Underwear."

"Boxer, brief, or bikini?"

"What? Uh . . . boxer."

"No."

"Yes."

"No. I mean, boxers won't do. Bikinis. In dark colors. Green to highlight your eyes. Blue to—"

"You're joking, right?"

"The Fortune Man wears sexy underwear, Taylor."

"Who's going to know what kind of underwear he—I'm—wearing?"

She smiled up at him. "You get a certain feeling wearing sexy underwear. Even if no one knows. It creates a mood, gives you an aura. And a hint of wickedness in your eyes."

Taylor's throat felt dry as his eyes strayed down Ali's sultry body, clad in an oversize polo shirt and jeans. Suddenly, all he could think about was what kind of underwear she wore.

Ali was well aware what he was thinking. One thing about Taylor, his face read like an open book. "Silk, Taylor. I'm wild about silk."

He reddened, but then his eyes met hers, a disarming smile on his face. "Silk. Yes, silk suits you."

Now it was Ali's turn to feel her cheeks warm. Why did she have to go and satisfy his curiosity? To prove his curiosity had no effect on her? No effect? So how come her heart was racing? How come her palms were sweaty? How come she was overcome by the impulse to throw herself into his arms? What was it about these Fortune boys, anyway?

She tried to get back to business. "Anyway, maybe we'll have you go public. All kinds of superstars are doing underwear commercials these days, Taylor. It could make for some fabulous press. The Fortune Man in a pair of sexy green bikini underpants."

"You're not serious."

"Taylor, Taylor, get this straight. I'm always serious when it comes to my work. You need help, Taylor." She briskly checked her watch. "Damn, we're late. Come on. We'll have to hurry."

"Where are we going?" Taylor asked as she grabbed his arm.

"To my hairdresser."

"Hairdresser?"

"Henri. He can do wonders." She grinned, eyeing Taylor's shaggy locks. "Trust me."

"IT'S SO NICE TO SEE YOU again, Ben," Jessica said demurely as she greeted the neuropsychiatrist in her front parlor.

Ben Engel rose as she entered. "You look surprised. Don't you know yet that I can never stay away from you for too long?"

"Ben Engel, you just love to see me blush."

"This, too, is true," he said, folding her hand between his.

"Are you staying long?" she asked, trying not to sound overeager, her gaze straying to his strong, capable, blue-veined hand resting over hers.

"I announced my retirement at the hospital yesterday."

"Ben, you finally did it."

"It's enough, Jess. I feel it is all right to have some time for myself—for a personal life—while I'm still not too old to enjoy it."

Jessica smiled ruefully. "You're not the one that's old."

He gave her a wiseacre grin. "And neither are you. Are you going to always rub it in that you're a little bit older than me?"

Jessica smiled gently. "Always."

They stared at each other for a long moment. Then they sat down together on the sofa. "So, tell me," Ben said, "how are the lovebirds doing?"

Jessica smiled. "Which ones?"

Ben laughed. "All of them. You must be thrilled to have them all back together in Denver. Adam and Eve, Peter and Elizabeth, Tru and Sasha. By the way, I spoke with the head of neuropsychiatry at Denver General this morning. He's going to offer Elizabeth the position."

Jessica beamed. "Oh, Ben, that is wonderful news. Now Peter can set up his haberdashery headquarters here as he'd wanted. I do think, for it all, Denver's in his blood. And the same for Adam and Tru, too. This is still home for them. Which couldn't delight me more."

"Those boys of yours are extraordinary, Jess. It's quite something to see how well they've succeeded without their inheritance."

"It's love, Ben. When you're in love anything is possible. There's just no stopping you when you've got the right person by your side."

"Yes," Ben said softly. "I believe that's true, Jess."

She gave him a distracted smile. "That's why—" She stopped, pursing her lips.

Ben knew that smile of hers only too well. "So it's Taylor now?"

"There's a woman, Ben. Why, she's Taylor made for him," she said with a sly smile.

"I see," he replied warily.

Jessica laughed, reaching out for his hand. "You know I won't be truly content until all four boys are settled."

"But you have told me that if Taylor marries, too, the family would lose Fortune's altogether. All the shares would go to Nolan Fielding."

"I'm sure Nolan will manage."

"That's not what I mean, Jess, and you know it. Do you really want to see everything your son, Alexander, built and left to his sons taken away?"

Jessica didn't answer right away. First she rose and poured two glasses of sherry from a crystal decanter. She handed a glass to Ben and then sat down again, sipping her sherry. "I loved my son, Ben. I loved him deeply. But I feel it was wrong of him to create this tontine. I say if we must sacrifice for something in this life, let it be for love. Not bricks, glass, shelves stocked with goods. You see yourself how well the others have done. Success, when it's hand in hand with love, is sweet, Ben. But success without love will ultimately leave a bitter taste in the mouth."

Ben tenderly touched Jessica's cheek. She pressed her hand over his.

"I've always worried the most about Taylor," Jessica said. "Ever since he was a boy he's been overshadowed by his three older brothers. Adam was so suave and charming, Peter so solid, reliable, and strong, Tru so exciting and reckless."

"Taylor has his special qualities, too."

"Oh, I know he does, Ben. He may not have the style, but he has substance. Unfortunately, most women don't take the time—"

"But this woman who is Taylor made . . . ?"

Jessica smiled impishly. "The minute I met Ali Spencer," she said, "I knew she was the one for Taylor. She has such life in her, Ben. She's vibrant, confident, bursting with crackling energy. You spend five minutes with her and you can almost see sparks shooting off her skin. And she has heart, Ben. She wears it on her sleeve—only she doesn't know it."

"And so you arranged a meeting?"

Jessica explained about Homer and how she'd encouraged Taylor to hire Ali as his publicist. "He was overwhelmed by her at first. But bedazzled, as well. Oh, I've never seen him like this before."

As if on cue, Taylor appeared in the doorway to the front parlor. At first Ben didn't recognize him. Even Jessica did a double take. "Taylor?"

He might have stepped out of a boating spread in a men's fashion magazine. His newly trimmed hair was combed fashionably back from his face and his lanky frame was outfitted in a stylish blue-and-white striped sailor's jersey and tapered white duck trousers. The slightly abstracted look in his hazel eyes was gone. He stood there with a half self-conscious, half roguish grin, his boyishness suddenly mixed with a can-do masculinity.

"Ali and I are going sailing," he announced with aplomb. "I just stopped by to let you know I'd be gone for the day."

"Sailing?" Jessica gave her grandson a bemused smile. "Here in Denver?"

"No. We're—uh—taking the company plane over to San Francisco. Adam's got a sloop docked there."

"So you're a sailor," Ben commented.

"Well, not exactly," Taylor hedged, then broke into a wide smile. "To tell you the truth, Dr. Engel, I haven't been on a boat since I was about nineteen. But Ali thinks . . . Well, she seems to feel it's important that I present a certain . . . rugged, seafaring image. It's the image that sells, you know."

"Ah," Ben said, glancing surreptitiously over at Jessica. "The image. I see."

"COME ON, TAYLOR. Take a deep breath," Ali soothed, although she was dismayed to see Taylor's coloring turn to somewhere between green and gray. She could forget about her camera. This wasn't exactly the image of The Fortune Man she wanted to pass on to the media.

Taylor was gripping the side of the boat. He made an attempt to follow Ali's advice, but it failed. "I think maybe . . . we should . . . go back to port."

"We've only been out for twenty minutes. You just need a little time to get your sea legs."

He clutched his stomach as the sailboat rose, then dipped over another swell. "It isn't my legs that are the problem, Ali."

Ali felt a twinge of guilt for feeling so damn healthy and vigorous when poor Taylor was in such agony. Being on the open sea was exhilarating for her. And she'd hoped it would put a little zing into Taylor. He'd looked downright glamorous—until they'd left the dock. She rested a sympathetic hand on his shoulder. "Maybe we should have started with tennis."

"I should have told you that the last time I went out on a boat I was horribly seasick. I was hoping I'd...outgrown it."

"Maybe if you try to focus on how to handle the jib . . ."

But even before she could finish the sentence, Taylor was heaving over the side of the boat. To add insult to injury, when they docked back at the boat basin and Ali was helping a wobbly, pale Taylor out of the boat, a photographer for the *San Francisco Sentinel* snapped his picture. This was not exactly the kind of publicity that would enhance the new image of The Fortune Man.

"I'M SORRY ABOUT THIS afternoon, Ali." They were back in Denver, sitting at the kitchen table of Ali's apartment. Sara had made a brief entrance, then had taken off for the evening.

"You'll be a lot sorrier in a few minutes. Unlike Sara, I make the world's worst coffee."

Taylor smiled. He was feeling much better. "Don't say that. You're a good cook. The dinner was great."

"It was takeout, Taylor. While you were resting I ran down to the little trattoria on the corner."

"Well, you made a great selection. The veal was wonderful. And the pasta was just great."

She smiled. "Didn't upset your stomach again?"

He smiled back. "I feel like a new man." He leaned forward. "You probably won't believe this, but I can't remember when I've had so much fun."

Ali stared at the percolating coffee, smiling to herself. "I can believe it."

"I've been wanting to ask you . . ." He hesitated.

"Ask me what?"

"Well, Eve—that's my sister-in-law . . ."

"I know. Adam and Eve. I followed their romance in the media. And Pete's. And Tru's. Something tells me that tontine of your father's backfired." She got up from the table and poured very dark-looking coffee into two mugs. She set one mug in front of Taylor. "So, what about Eve?"

"She's having a party. Well, sort of a celebration. For Homer. Just the family. Well . . . And friends. Some friends. Not too many. It's not really a big party."

"I'd love to go, Taylor."

"You would?"

"Sure. A celebration for Homer? Why, Homer and I are like that." She held up two crossed fingers and they both laughed.

Taylor sipped his coffee. It was probably the worst coffee he'd ever tasted. He glanced over the rim to see her watching him expectantly.

"Well?" she asked. "Was I right? About the coffee?"

He grinned at her. "I'll bet you're rarely wrong about anything, Ali Spencer."

4

THE THREE BROTHERS gathered in the den of Adam and Eve's split-level apartment in downtown Denver on the afternoon of the party.

"I don't like it," Pete said, eyeing Adam.

"Look, don't blame me," Adam replied. "I doubt this little celebration was all Eve's doing. She's been on the phone practically around the clock with both Lizzy and Sasha, making plans, discussing the guest list—"

"Don't call her Lizzy," Pete snapped. "You know she hates the nickname."

"Well, then, don't go accusing Eve of playing match-maker," Adam countered irritably.

Pete glared at Adam. "Well, whatever you want to call the game..."

Tru, who was wolfing down a handful of honey-roasted cashews, stepped in between his two brothers. "Come on, guys. This isn't solving anything. It doesn't matter if Eve planned this party or Liz—Elizabeth. The point is—"

"Hold on, Tru. Let's not forget Sasha," Adam said, cutting him off.

"Yes, don't think Sasha's just an innocent bystander," Pete interjected.

Tru raised his eyebrows. "Okay, okay. I'm willing to bet the three of them were in on this together. Women are such impossible romantics."

Adam and Pete nodded solemnly in agreement.

Tru returned to his cashews, Pete sipped his gin and tonic and Adam stared reflectively down at his new Persian carpet. Ever since this Ali Spencer business began, the three brothers had all been feeling tense and irritable. And it wasn't helping matters any that their wives, like their grandmother, all thought it would be wonderful if Taylor found himself a mate. And all four women seemed to agree that Ali Spencer would fit the bill very nicely.

After a while, Adam said, "Did you hear she threw out all his clothes?"

The other two hooted.

"Taylor told Eve that Ali's outfitting him with a whole new wardrobe," Adam continued.

"And Taylor's just going along with this?" Tru asked.

"He told Eve that Ali felt his image lacked pizzazz."

"Pizzazz?" Pete shook his head in amazement.

"How come Taylor's telling Eve all this?" Tru asked.

"Taylor's always felt comfortable confiding in Eve," Adam reflected. "I remember when they first met he showed her Homer before he even showed the robot to any of us."

"What else has he told her?" Pete demanded warily.

"Are you ready for this?" Adam paused dramatically, and both of his brothers inhaled a breath as if to cushion the news they were about to receive. "Ali's teaching him how to drive."

"Taylor?" both brothers exclaimed in unison.

Adam smiled wryly. "Well, not Homer, guys. Although, if you ask me, I'd rather see that robot behind the wheel than our baby brother."

"STOP SIGN. SLOW DOWN. No, no, stay over to your right. Okay. Brake, Taylor. Brake." Ali white-knuckled the dashboard as the car jerked and bucked. "No, that's the clutch, Taylor." Her raspy voice was unusually high-pitched. Panic did that to her. She had broken out into a sweat, partly due

to the afternoon heat hovering low over the city, partly due
to nerves. After a half hour of sitting here with Taylor behind the wheel of her Subaru hatchback, a car she'd grown
particularly fond of these past three years, she felt a new-
found empathy for driving instructors. Surely they had to
have the patience of Job. Her patience, on the other hand, was
close to running on empty.

"Sorry," Taylor muttered, as the car jerked. "Brake. Middle pedal. There," he said nervously, coming to a dead stop.
Unfortunately, he was three feet beyond the stop sign and into
the intersection, with cars honking and whizzing around him.

Then, in his haste to get across the road, he stalled the car.
Par for the afternoon's hair-raising course.

"No, stop giving it gas, Taylor. You're flooding the en-
gine."

He glanced over at her. "You're upset, aren't you?"

Ali did her best to plaster on a smile, but it came off as a
pained grimace. "Hey, this kind of thing happens to all new
drivers. Maybe we should have started on an automatic."

A minute later, much to Ali's relief, Taylor managed to get
the car started. She shuddered as he stripped through the
gears, silently apologizing to her dear little Subaru; but at
least they were moving again.

"Okay, now you want to prepare to make a left turn at the
next corner," Ali said, trying to keep her voice calm and even-
tempered. "No. No. Don't change lanes yet. Just slow down
a little, check your side- and rearview mirrors. No. Too much
brake, Taylor. You'll have the car behind you slamming right
into your—"

Before she finished the sentence, the car behind them
slammed right into their rear fender. Ali was afraid to turn
around. Taylor, who'd checked in the rearview mirror,
thought it was just as well that she didn't look. The car that
had run into them was a Denver police cruiser. . . .

"I DON'T KNOW, SARA. Maybe this time I've bitten off more than I can chew," Ali despaired, reemerging from the refrigerator with a cooked chicken leg. "I guess I had this fantasy that all Taylor needed was a good haircut, some classy clothes, and everything else would fall into place." She bit off a piece of meat and chewed. "So far, thanks to my Fortune Man, I've got a ruined nightgown—"

"He did replace it with a new one that was absolutely divine."

But Ali wasn't listening. "A smashed-in rear fender, and a two-hundred-dollar fine for having no brakelights. I know those lights were working just fine before Taylor got behind the wheel. I swear, he jinxed my car."

"Come on, Ali. The guy's an electronics whiz. He built Homer, didn't he?"

Ali eyed her ruefully. "I rest my case."

"Now, wait a minute. So Homer went a little haywire. You were in his way when he was trying to change the linens. Speaking of which, did you see the way that robot made your bed? And washed our kitchen floor? If I had the dough I'd buy myself a Homer in a minute."

Ali sighed. "It's not Homer I'm worried about at the moment. It's Taylor. He's just so . . . out of touch. So awkward. So . . ."

"Sweet? So endearing? So uncomplicated?" Sara plucked the chicken leg from Ali's hand and waved it at her. "What about Taylor being a breath of fresh air?"

Ali grabbed the chicken leg back and took another bite out of it. "You're forgetting. I'm a New Yorker. I can take just so much fresh air."

"Well," Sara said philosophically, "think of yourself as Rex Harrison and Taylor as Audrey Hepburn."

"Huh?"

"You know. Professor Higgins. Eliza Doolittle. *My Fair Lady*?"

Ali was about to make a snide remark about reality being a little more complex than the movies, but then she gave the film some more thought. She really could identify with Professor Higgins. And she thought about the key to his success. Persistence. That was it. Frustrated and despairing though he may have been on many an occasion with the irrepressible cockney flower girl, Higgins refused to give up. And why? Not so much the wager he made with his old friend, but a point of pride. He refused to fail at the task. Besides, it was an incredible challenge. Was she forgetting that she loved just such a challenge herself? Wasn't The Fortune Man transformation a point of pride for her? Hadn't she learned long ago that persistence always paid off in the end?

She grabbed up her pocketbook and started toward the front door.

"Where are you going?" Sara called out.

"I'm going to buy a dozen pairs of bikini underpants," Ali shouted back.

Sara popped her head out the kitchen door. "But didn't you buy yourself a whole batch of new underwear just a few weeks ago?"

Ali turned around and tossed the finished chicken bone down the hall to Sara. "Men's bikinis," she said with a wink.

ALI GAVE HER COPPER CURLS a derisive sneer. It was the one element of her appearance that refused to cooperate with the sharp, self-possessed, go-get-'em public image she had carefully created and honed over the years. What she wouldn't give for a head of stick-straight wheat-colored hair streaked with creamy natural-blond flashes. It was tough to be a high-powered publicist when you had a head of hair that reminded most clients of Little Orphan Annie. Not that she hadn't learned how to overcome her disability. She'd worked hard over the past six years in the business figuring out how to project an aura of surefire confidence, even when she was quaking in her boots. And she had an ambush approach to her job that left the unsuspecting in awe. She was a good talker, and she knew it and used it. After a while people forgot about her cartoon-cute hair and simply saw a five-foot-seven-inch twenty-eight-year-old dynamo who knew how to take charge of a client, a product and a situation, and did precisely that. Ali was in good shape as long as she was in control. It was when that control started to slip that she was in trouble. It didn't happen very often. But Ali knew that trouble had been nipping at her heels ever since she'd first set eyes on Taylor Fortune and dreamed up The Fortune Man.

"Hey, your Fortune Man's chauffeur is at the door," Sara said brightly, from the doorway of Ali's room. "It's party time."

Ali donned one of her go-get-'em expressions. "Didn't Taylor come?"

Sara shook her head. "You look great, Ali. New dress?" she asked, admiring the mint green silk shantung cocktail dress. "That color goes fabulously with your hair."

Ali glowered. "Don't talk about my hair." She grabbed up her beaded purse. "And why isn't Taylor here?"

"He's probably getting Homer spiffed up for the party," Sara teased. "Don't tell me you're nervous walking into the party alone? Hey, you've got an in with one Fortune. What's five or six more Fortunes, give or take a Fortune here or there?"

"Very funny," Ali said distractedly as she looked around the room.

"What's missing?"

"My camera."

"You're not taking pictures at the party?"

"Are you kidding?" Ali countered. "An intimate bash thrown by the fabulous Fortune boys for their kid brother and heir to the Fortune dynasty? This will kick off my Fortune Man campaign. Taylor, decked out in a Pierre Cardin dinner jacket, white silk shirt—"

"And don't forget the black bikini underpants," Sara interrupted with a grin. "Although I guess you won't really know if he's wearing them. Or will you find out after the party's over?"

Ali laughed. A fake laugh, but a laugh nonetheless. "Forget it. Even if I didn't have strict rules about messing around with clients, Taylor Fortune is definitely not my type—a breath of fresh air notwithstanding." She spied her camera half-hidden under a pile of clothes on a chair in the corner of her room and snatched it up. "My limo awaits."

Eve WAS EFFUSIVE in her greeting as she met Ali at the door. But then she asked, "Where's Taylor?"

"Isn't he here?" Ali replied, an uncharacteristic edge of nervousness in her voice.

"No," Eve said, biting on her lower lip. But then she immediately brightened as she whisked Ali inside. "I'm sure he'll be along soon. He's probably testing Homer out to make sure there'll be no further embarrassing incidents."

"He told you about my incident with Homer?"

Eve smiled. "I wheedled it out of him after he corralled me into helping him pick out a silk nightie, size seven."

Ali felt her cheeks warm, but Eve put a friendly arm around her shoulder. "Poor Taylor. He was so embarrassed," she said, taking the focus off Ali.

Ali relaxed a little. She liked Eve. She hoped she'd feel the same about the others.

There were about twenty people at the party, all milling about Adam and Eve Fortune's posh, airy two-story living

room whose floor-to-ceiling windows looked out on a spectacular city vista with a mountain backdrop. Jessica Fortune
approached Ali as Eve guided her into the room.

"It's lovely to see you here, Ali," Jessica said warmly, taking hold of her hand.

"It's nice to see you again, Mrs. Fortune."

The two women shared a smile. Ali was well aware that she
had Taylor's grandmother to thank for opening the door for
her to get the Homer account. Jessica Fortune had come to
see her at her office a few weeks back to discuss Homer. At
the time, Ali had been so excited about the possibility of such
an account that she never once considered that the older
woman might have an ulterior motive. But now she wasn't
so sure Jessica Fortune hadn't intended all along for her to take
Taylor, and not Homer, in hand. For what end? That was the
sixty-four-thousand-dollar question.

Before Ali had any time to ponder it, she was greeted by
two more Fortune wives, Sasha and Elizabeth. Both women
gave her enthusiastic welcomes, although they, too, seemed
a little concerned that Taylor hadn't arrived with her.

"Maybe we should give Taylor a call," Elizabeth suggested, her eyes straying in the direction of her husband, Pete,
who was standing near a window talking to Adam and Tru.

Eve followed her sister-in-law's gaze and frowned faintly.
"Good idea. I'll give him a buzz."

Jessica nodded, slipping her arm through Ali's. "I'll introduce Ali around." As they started off, Ali had the distinct
feeling that Jessica Fortune deliberately maneuvered her away
from the three Fortune brothers.

"GRAN'S BRINGING HER over now," Tru said under his breath.
"It's about time."

"We're relying on you, Adam," Pete murmured.

"Don't worry. Leave it to me," Adam replied confidently.

The three brothers all plastered pleasant smiles on their faces as Ali approached. Ali did the same, but she was certain their smiles were as fake as hers. Ever since she'd walked into this party she'd been aware of their covert glances in her direction.

After a few minutes of awkward chitchat, Adam, who hadn't lost his touch, managed to steer Ali off to a quiet corner of the room for a little talk. As soon as he took off with Ali, Pete and Tru sprang into action, their task being to keep the Fortune women from interrupting while Adam had his little heart-to-heart with the publicist.

Adam intended to build up his pitch, but Ali gave him a knowing look.

"How about cutting right to the chase?" she said bluntly as soon as they were out of earshot of the other partygoers.

Adam grinned. "My brother warned me you were very direct."

"Taylor?" Ali looked edgy.

"No. Pete."

"Oh." Ali relaxed a little.

"Tell me, Ali, what do you think of Taylor?"

"What do I think of him?" she echoed. So much for relaxation.

"Okay, I won't beat around the bush. My brothers and I feel that this idea of yours to promote Taylor as . . ."

Ali arched a brow. "The Fortune Man?"

"Right. Well, it isn't such a good idea."

"Taylor told me none of you have much confidence in his robot, and to be perfectly frank, Adam, I have my doubts about Homer, myself. But Homer isn't the point. By publicizing Taylor, everything his company sells will take on added glitter, added appeal. I predict that sales figures will climb right across the board, once I get this campaign rolling. I know I'm tooting my own horn, but I do think it's a fantastic marketing strategy. Not that it's a totally original idea. Other CEOs have been marketed to plug their companies, but Taylor's situation—thanks to this tontine business—is unique."

"Yes, the tontine," Adam emphasized, as if to remind her that Taylor was not an eligible bachelor.

Ali missed the point of his remark. And would probably have been utterly surprised to know that Adam and his brothers were actually afraid Taylor's claim to the tontine might be in jeopardy. Marrying Taylor was the farthest thing from her mind. At the moment. "And the tontine makes Taylor unique," she responded enthusiastically, hoping to win Adam's support for her plan. "Which, in turn, makes for great copy."

"I suppose," Adam said acerbically, "that depends on whether the copy lands on the front pages or the comics page."

Ali gave him a sharp look. "Which means?"

"Come on, Ali. You've spent enough time now with Taylor to know he's not exactly the kind of guy who fits the picture of the suave, cosmopolitan man-about-town. Which, I assume, is how you envision The Fortune Man." Condescension seeped into Adam's voice.

Ali stiffened. "Okay, maybe he's not exactly ideal for the role. But there is potential here."

"We don't want to see Taylor being made a laughingstock, Ali. And we think there's potential here for that."

"We, meaning you and your brothers?"

Adam nodded. "Yes. We think Taylor's going to have a difficult enough time handling the running of Fortune's without added pressures or . . . distractions."

"You don't have much faith in Taylor, do you? You or your brothers?"

"Now, wait a second—"

"No. We don't need to waste any more time. I have the picture, Adam. But since Taylor is in charge, I think it's up to him to decide what pressures or 'distractions' he can handle."

"Listen, Ali—"

"I don't intend to have Taylor become a laughingstock, Adam. All he needs is a bit of polishing and—"

"It isn't only that, Ali. Look, the guy's got a—" But Adam didn't finish his sentence. His mouth dropped open as he stared off toward the other side of the living room. A hush had abruptly come over the gathering. Ali slowly turned her head and followed Adam's gaze. Then her mouth dropped open.

There was Taylor standing in the entryway, his hair on end, his face streaked with black smudges, his brand-new white dinner jacket looking as if it had gotten caught in a lion's jaw.

"I'm fine, everyone," Taylor said to the gaping faces, breaking the stunned silence. "I just had a bit of a problem with Homer in the elevator. A…faulty circuit. I'm afraid he's not exactly in any condition for a celebration." Taylor's eyes searched the room until they landed on Ali. He gave her a wistful smile. There were other smiling faces, too. The Fortune women were smiling sympathetically in her direction. And the Fortune brothers all regarded her now with "I told you" smiles.

Ali didn't smile back at any of them. Nor was she the least inclined to snap any photos of her Fortune Man.

"YOU DIDN'T HAVE A VERY good time tonight, did you?"

Ali shifted in the back seat of the limo and looked out the window. "It was fine."

He cupped her chin, forcing her to face him. "I'm sorry, Ali. I know I was pretty distracted all evening."

"Distracted? Taylor, you hardly spoke to a soul all evening. You spent most of your time sitting in a corner, scribbling...."

"I was just trying to figure out a solution to the problem I'm having with Homer."

Ali took in a breath. "Listen to me, Taylor. You've got to make an effort here. Your brothers all seem to think it's hopeless trying to promote you as The Fortune Man."

"They do?"

Ali gave him a level look. "Maybe they're right, Taylor. Maybe you ought to rethink your decision to go along with my plan." She couldn't believe she was saying this. She could feel her golden opportunity slipping like sand through her fingers.

"Is that what you're doing?" he asked quietly.

Ali couldn't quite meet his gaze.

"Do you want me to let you off the hook, Ali?" There was a note of vulnerability in Taylor's voice. It touched Ali. She looked up into his warm hazel eyes.

"No," she said in a low voice. "I want to let you off the hook. If you want off."

"I don't want off." He leaned a little closer to her, blushing. "I'm even wearing those black bikinis."

Ali's gaze lowered reflexively, but then, embarrassed, she quickly turned away.

"Look, Taylor, tonight was a bust—" she addressed the window "—but we'll just put it aside, forget about it."

"You look beautiful in that dress, Ali."

She shut her eyes.

"You should have seen me before I got into that elevator with Homer tonight. I looked pretty spiffy, if I do say so myself."

Ali turned back to him and grinned. "You sure made a grand entrance."

"I had every eye in the room on me. That was the idea—sort of." He smiled.

She smiled back. "You do have potential, Taylor. I don't care what your brothers think."

He couldn't take his eyes off her. "I wanted to dance with you tonight."

"All you had to do was ask."

"I don't dance very well. When I was about fourteen my grandmother enrolled me in dance school. You know—ballroom dancing for social occasions. We all went through it in turn. Adam, Pete, Tru and I. Adam was a natural. Pete was diligent. Tru got booted out for playing disco music."

"And you?" Ali asked.

"I stepped on so many girls' shoes that I think they all got together and signed a petition to have me ousted."

"You're joking."

Taylor smiled. "Only about the petition. I did step on dozens of patent-leather shoes. And I was asked politely to leave. The dance teacher felt I was just not cut out for ballroom dancing."

"That's ridiculous. I'm sure I could teach you to dance," she said spontaneously, forgetting all about her earlier frustrating efforts to teach him to drive.

"DID I HURT YOU?"

Ali looked down at her scuffed pumps and stepped away from Taylor. "How about if we start with a fox-trot instead of a waltz?"

They were in the living room of the carriage house on the Fortune estate that Taylor had converted into his apartment and work space. Ali crossed the large, sparsely furnished loftlike room to examine his collection of CDs. There was a surprisingly eclectic mix of classical, jazz and blues—and even some contemporary rock music.

"What? No bagpipe music?" she teased as he came up behind her.

"Not on CD. I have some on tape."

"I think we'd better concentrate on the fox-trot before we
move on to the Highland fling."

Taylor grinned. "You're the teacher."

She popped in a Billie Holiday CD, and turned to step into
Taylor's arms.

He hesitated, feeling a surge of nerves. It wasn't that he
didn't want to hold her in his arms, feel her body pressed up
against his as they swayed to the melodic strains of a romantic bluesy Holiday number. It was that he wanted it too much.
It was his desire far more than his two left feet that kept him
from concentrating on her instruction.

"What is it? Don't you like this tune?" Ali asked.

"Maybe we can . . . sit this one out," he muttered.

Ali was aware of Taylor's uneasiness, but she assumed it
was merely his feeling of inadequacy about his dancing.
"Look, it just takes practice. Don't be discouraged. You'll get
the knack of it. Why, before I'm through, I'll have women
fighting to have you sign their dance cards," she teased.
"You'll have women falling all over you, Taylor."

"Is that the goal?"

Ali picked up on the edge in his voice. "The goal is to make
The Fortune Man a household word." She checked her
watch. "It's getting late. I guess we'll have to schedule another lesson some other time. I should go."

Impulsively, he took her into his arms, his face set with a
stubborn resoluteness. "No. Let's dance. It just takes practice, right?"

The moment Taylor took her in his arms a little alarm went
off in Ali's head. Yes, the goal was to have women falling all
over him. Every woman but her, that was. She had to keep
her perspective. Stay in control. Keep her distance. Which

wasn't easy when she was pressed up against his lean, attractive, very appealing body. . . .

This time she stepped on his toe.

"You're not concentrating," he teased. "It's a simple box step, remember. Step forward on your right foot, then slide it to the right—"

She drew back. "It really is late, Taylor. We both need our beauty sleep."

He smiled at her. "You don't." He rather forcefully pulled her back into his arms. "Besides, I think I'm beginning to get the hang of it."

She chastised herself for having so rashly offered this after-hours dance class. It was definitely not a good idea. Instead of her teaching Taylor the fox-trot, he was teaching her that her body could go haywire in his arms.

"You're trembling, Ali."

"I'm tired, Taylor. That's all. Just tired. I've been working hard and . . ."

He stopped dancing and looked down at her. "How come there isn't a man in your life, Ali?"

"What?"

"You're so smart, so pretty, so talented. How come some guy hasn't come along by now and snatched you up?"

"I've never wanted to be 'snatched up.'"

"I didn't mean it like that. I just mean . . . Haven't you ever been in love, Ali?"

She extricated herself from his arms, stepping away until she felt she was at a safe distance. "Now look, Taylor. I should be the one asking you these questions. After all, I'm the publicist. These are the kinds of facts I need to know about you in order to work—"

"No."

"No?"

"No, I've never been in love. Mostly, I guess, I've been indifferent."

Ali hesitated. "There's never been anyone whom you've even . . . ?"

Taylor smiled. "I said mostly. Not entirely."

Ali nodded quickly and awkwardly. "I didn't mean— Well, it's none of my business."

"What about you?"

"What about . . . me? Me and men, you mean?"

"I guess you've had your share of experiences."

"Well, I have had a few . . . involvements. But—"

"But you've never been in love?"

"I'm afraid I'm a bit too much of a cynic for love."

"Did someone once hurt you?" Taylor asked bluntly.

"No. Not exactly."

She folded her arms across her chest, trying to think of some way to shift the conversation off such a personal topic.

"I'm making you uncomfortable. I don't mean to pry, Ali. I'm just interested. I'd like to know more about you."

"You're turning the tables on me here, Taylor. I'm the one that's supposed to be asking the questions." She looked nervously around the room. "This is a great space."

Taylor smiled. He knew she was angling to be let off the hook. "I guess it is. I don't spend much time here." He, too, looked around. "I guess it isn't exactly decorated in Fortune Man fashion."

"Well, this is your private domain—"

"No, it should reflect my new image. The image we're working on, I should say. I know I still need plenty of coaching. If you have any suggestions—about the decorating . . ."

"Oh, I do. I mean, I could offer a few ideas."

"I guess setting is important."

"Right. We could so some redecorating and then I could do a spread of The Fortune Man at home."

"Maybe I could have Homer doing some chores and we could have some other prime merchandise from Fortune's casually scattered around the room."

"That's a great idea, Taylor." Ali felt more in control now. She was back in her element. She'd just gotten briefly sidetracked. "We might even have you throw a little party. Only this time you have to promise, no tinkering."

Taylor's gaze swung over to the couch where his tattered, stained dinner jacket had been tossed. He grinned. "I promise."

A new song came on, a slow, bluesy Billie Holiday torch song. Taylor held his arms out. "One more before we say good-night? Just to see if I'm catching on?"

Something told her he was catching on faster than she'd ever expected—maybe faster than she could handle.

5

ALI WAS JUST ABOUT to slip into bed when her phone rang. Who could be calling at close to one in the morning?

"Hi. I didn't wake you, did I?"

"Taylor? Is that you? What's the noise in the background?"

"Oh. Bagpipes. I told you I had bagpipe music."

"I did believe you, Taylor."

"Ali?" He switched the receiver to his other hand, sat down on the edge of his bed, and then stood up again. "I couldn't sleep. You weren't asleep yet, were you?"

"No," Ali said softly, switching the receiver to her other hand, sitting down on the edge of her bed, then standing again.

"It was really great dancing with you tonight, Ali. I mean, I know I stepped on your toes a lot...."

"I stepped on your toes, too, Taylor. And I don't even have an excuse."

Taylor smiled. "I didn't mind."

Ali felt uneasy. "You're awfully sweet, Taylor. But, you know, you really do have to be careful not to let people step on your toes too often."

"I suppose you've got a point."

"I'm not talking about dancing now, Taylor."

"I know you're not, Ali."

"That includes me, too. I can be pushy, Taylor. I can be very pushy."

"You're assertive."

"I can be insensitive."

"You're focused."

"And I can be awfully demanding."

"Challenging. And awfully attractive."

"Oh, Taylor, what am I going to do with you? You turn everything around."

"You've turned everything around for me, too, Ali. Ever since I met you I feel like I've been in a state of constant motion."

"See. I told you. Pushy. Insensitive. Demanding. . . ."

"I kind of like the feeling."

Ali sank down on her bed, slowly stretching out.

Across town, Taylor did precisely the same thing.

There was a long silence.

"Ali? Are you still there?"

"Yes, Taylor."

They both shut their eyes. There was another silence.

"Ali. It's hard for me to say things. At times like this I wish I were more like my brothers. Adam is so smooth and charming. He's always able to say the right things at the right time. To women, especially. And Pete's so clear minded, knows just what he wants and goes after it. And then there's Tru. Oh, he'd fight his feelings like crazy, but he'd do it in such a sexy, irrepressible way that you wouldn't be able to resist him."

"They've all got a distinctive style, Taylor. I'll grant you that. But you've got your own inimitable appeal." No sooner had the words come out of her mouth than she sprang up in bed, realizing that the conversation and her feelings were getting way out of hand. "What I mean, Taylor . . . What I'm saying is that . . ."

"Yes, Ali?" Taylor sat up, too.

"Look, Taylor, what I'm trying to say is that while you have some . . . wonderful qualities . . ."

"Do I, Ali?"

"Yes. Yes, you do, Taylor. But...they're not necessarily the qualities that . . . for publicity purposes . . . sell products. Do you follow what I'm saying?"

"I think so."

"We need to put in some hard work in the next few weeks, developing your new image."

"The Fortune Man."

"Yes, exactly. By the end of the month, Taylor, you will be The Fortune Man."

"It means a lot to you, doesn't it?"

"It means a lot to both of us, Taylor."

"I hope I won't disappoint you, Ali. I'll really try to put my best foot forward. And not let it land on anyone's toes."

Ali sank back down on her bed. "And I'll try to do the same. If I do accidentally step on your toes again, Taylor..."

"I'll let you know if it hurts, Ali," he said, stretching back down on his bed.

They both hung up at the same time and sighed deeply.

WHEN ALI SPOTTED Taylor arriving at the Marley Art Gallery the next evening, she breathed a sigh of relief. He was unsmudged, his snappy new Italian designer suit intact, his hair stylishly combed. Indeed, he looked incredibly urbane. And incredibly handsome.

Taylor, too, wore a look of relief when he saw Ali, but when he started in her direction she surreptitiously shook her head. The point, as he already knew, was to mingle and be charming with the rich, arty, society set who were here for the New Wave show opening. Ali, her small Nikon camera in hand, was there simply to record The Fortune Man in operation.

A young woman with short blond hair moussed at the front into an exotic wave approached Taylor, giving him a "Should I know you?" sort of look. As soon as he introduced himself, her heart-shaped face lit up.

"Well, Taylor Fortune, how fortunate to run into you like this," she murmured coyly, snatching up a couple of glasses of champagne from a nearby table and handing him one of them. Taylor gave the goblet an uneasy look and deposited it back on the table.

"Last time I drank champagne I pretty much made a complete fool of myself," he confessed.

Ali, who had edged her way through the crowd and was standing nearby, pretending to snap photos of some of the sculptures, winced as she overheard Taylor's remark.

The blonde, whom Ali had recognized as socialite gossip columnist Jill Barnett, batted her big blue eyes at Taylor. "You just tell me all about it," she simpered, slipping her arm through his.

Ali had to do something. She spied an art patron, Vanessa Milnar, chatting with one of the New Wave artists. Maneuvering her way right behind them, she muttered sotto voce, "Well, I'll be— If it isn't Taylor Fortune! I wonder if he's in the market to buy."

Before Vanessa turned around to see who had made the comment, Ali had slipped off, melting into the crowd.

Less than a minute later, Vanessa, her young artist in tow, was whisking Taylor away from a pouting Jill Barnett, who'd only just begun to get any useful tidbits for her column.

Ali watched Vanessa introduce Taylor to several other artists, all of whom were participating in the evening's New Wave opening. No doubt Vanessa was hoping to encourage the wealthy young bachelor to become a patron of the arts. They were heading toward a large, rather grotesque, multi-sectioned moon-shaped sculpture covered with brass nuggets. Ali was all set to position herself nearby, camera at the ready, when she was waylaid by Steve Dennis, a fellow publicist from a competing Denver agency.

"Work or pleasure, Spencer?"

Ali was surprised the word hadn't yet leaked about her new assignment, but she was more than happy to keep it that way until her Fortune Man campaign was really off the ground.

"Oh, just free-lancing, Dennis," she said offhandedly, trying to discreetly keep her eye on Taylor. Unfortunately, a group moved into her line of vision, obscuring him from view.

She started off, but Steve Dennis draped a friendly arm around her shoulders. "You're looking great, Ali."

She disengaged his arm. This wasn't the first time the rival publicist had made a pass at her. Nor the first time she'd rebuffed him. They had it down to a well-rehearsed routine. "Thanks, Dennis. But shouldn't we mingle? I gather you're here on business, since I doubt this sort of art is your style."

Steve Dennis smiled crookedly. "You're right, beautiful. I've seen better etchings on subway stations. Speaking of etchings, what are you doing after you blow this joint?"

"Going home," she said firmly, trying to act nonchalant as she looked around the gallery for Taylor. At first she couldn't find him anywhere. But then she heard a commotion across the room. Both she and Steve Dennis turned to see a hapless, apologetic Taylor Fortune holding a piece of the moon sculpture with brass nuggets in his hand as the irate artist looked on aghast and then began accusing Taylor of deliberately defacing his art.

"But I only meant to point out that it looked unbalanced," Taylor tried to explain as a group began to gather. "I didn't realize it was so fragile."

Ali fought back a sigh.

"Say, isn't that one of the Fortune boys?" Steve Dennis murmured beside her. "Hey, it is. That's Taylor Fortune. I heard he was a real recluse. Wow, this could make great copy." He slipped his camera out of his jacket pocket just as Taylor accidentally clobbered Vanessa Milnar with the piece of sculpture in his efforts to rectify the damage.

Ali could just see the photo splashed on the front page of tomorrow's society column. Before Dennis had a chance to snap the picture, she whirled around, grabbing the amorous publicist's arm.

"So tell me, Dennis," she murmured seductively, "do you really have better etchings than this at home?" Once she got him to his place, she'd beg off with a headache.

The publicist hesitated, then smiled lecherously, slipping his camera back into his pocket.

Taylor, who'd been nervously searching the crowd for Ali, spotted her just as she and Dennis were leaving the gallery, arm in arm.

TAYLOR WAS SITTING on the doorstep outside Ali's building when she stepped out of the cab. He was happy to see that she was alone.

She hesitated before walking over. Taylor rose as she approached.

"Sorry I had to leave you in the lurch," she started to say, but Taylor cut her off.

"Ali, a man should know where he fits in."

"Taylor..."

"I just don't fit in at cocktail parties, dances, art openings—"

"Taylor..."

"I never seem to say or do the right things. I don't think I'm going to be able to carry this off."

Ali started to argue with him, set on convincing him otherwise, but in the end she said nothing and merely sat down on the concrete step.

"Who was the man? The one you left with?" There was no hiding the note of jealousy and disappointment in his voice.

She looked up at him, smiling crookedly. "That was no man, Taylor. That was a publicist."

Taylor sat down beside her. "Oh, a colleague."

"Only in the broadest sense. He works for the Younger agency. Our biggest competitors."

He turned to face her, observing her intently. "You seemed . . . friendly enough. But then, I suppose the two of you have a lot in common. And he's certainly a good-looking man. Seemed real sure of himself. Probably felt right at home at the opening. I guess he's the sort of man a woman like you would—"

"Run from at the first opportunity," she cut him off. "Except in an emergency. Which this was. I maneuvered Dennis out of there before he snapped a shot of that chunk of sculpture in your hand meeting up with Vanessa Milnar's head. How *is* her head, by the way? She isn't planning to sue you, I hope."

"I don't think so. She seemed okay. Just a little confused for a moment."

"You have that effect on women."

"Do I have that effect on you?"

Slowly, she nodded. "You're a foreign quantity to me, Taylor. I've never run across anyone like you before. I sometimes wonder if you're for real."

Their eyes searched each other's. Then Taylor did what she'd been telling herself for days she didn't want to want him to do: He kissed her. For a couple of moments before his lips met hers, she had the opportunity to object. And she knew that, as much as he wanted to kiss her, he would have pulled back. He would have respected her wishes. That was precisely what she meant about Taylor being a foreign quantity. He was one of the few men she'd met in her life who were givers rather than takers. If only she could find one major flaw in his character; something to convince her that he was like all the others—all the others she had so painstakingly avoided getting involved with. But she couldn't find that flaw.

So, as his lips moved toward hers, she didn't make a peep of protest. She even tilted her head up at just the right angle. And as their lips touched, she leaned into him, leaving no doubt in either of their minds as to what she was feeling.

Taylor had been utterly distraught earlier when he'd seen Ali taking off with that tall, handsome man, their arms linked. He had felt a rush of jealousy unlike anything he'd ever experienced. When she'd told him about her motive for dragging the publicist off, he'd felt like a man on death row who'd received an eleventh-hour pardon. *This is crazy!* he told himself. Ali was the last woman in the world for him to get involved with. For one thing, he was convinced she felt more pity than passion for him. What she wanted was The Fortune Man—someone suave, sophisticated, playful, self-assured; a man who always said and did the right things.

But still, as his lips met hers, he felt a rush of desire so strong it made him catch his breath. She was so soft and warm. She was so patient and sweet. She felt and smelled so good to him.

Despite all her best intentions, Ali gave herself up willingly to the kiss, her arms slipping around his neck. *This is crazy!* she told herself. But at the moment she just didn't care. She just wanted to kiss him, to go on kissing him.

It was Taylor who pulled away. He rose abruptly, knowing that if he didn't, he would kiss her again. And he wouldn't want to stop kissing her. He couldn't let himself get out of hand. Nor could he pretend that Ali really desired him in the way he desired her. She was just being kind. She probably felt sorry for him. That wasn't the basis for a relationship—not the kind of relationship he'd taken to having fantasies about.

"Good night, Ali." He started for the curb. Only then did Ali notice the limo parked across the street, and Taylor's chauffeur, Daniel, patiently sitting behind the wheel, staring discreetly ahead.

"Taylor," she called out to him.

He stopped a few feet from the curb and turned back to face her.

"What happened after I left the gallery?" she asked, playing for time, not sure why. "That dreadful artist didn't take a swing at you or anything?"

Taylor smiled. "No. I finally managed to calm him down."

Ali didn't hide her surprise. "You did? How?"

"I bought the sculpture."

"Oh, Taylor."

"And two of his paintings. One of them wasn't all that bad."

They both laughed, but then Taylor's expression turned serious. "The Fortune Man was a great idea, Ali," he said abruptly. "But what I came over tonight to tell you was that I'm just not the guy to pull it off." There, he'd told her. There was no getting away from the truth. Better to stop it now before her pity turned to frustration and disappointment.

Ali was dumbfounded. Surely he wasn't saying that he was calling off the deal? Was that what that kiss was all about? Goodbye? A current of panic rippled down her spine. No, he couldn't be serious.

Taylor was puzzled and dismayed by her silence. But perhaps it was for the best. It proved to him that she was honest enough not to try to persuade him he was wrong. He liked that about her. But it was better this way. A clean break. In time, his fantasies would stop. He hoped.

"I'm sorry, Ali." He turned and started to cross the street.

Impulsively, Ali sprang up from the concrete doorstep and rushed over to him, grabbing his arm. "Listen, Taylor. I think I've been pushing you too hard, too fast. You need a little more time, a little more practice before we launch the campaign. I have an idea." *Quick, Ali, before you lose him*, she told herself, not really sure she was only talking about losing a star client. "I have this little cottage—a kind of hideaway—just north of the city. About an hour's drive. Why don't we go up there for a few days, away from art shows and cocktail parties? We could unwind a little. I could give you some pointers, build up your self-confidence, we could work on some dance steps. You could call it a rehearsal."

Taylor stared at her, his expression thoughtful, but he didn't say anything.

Ali realized she was still gripping his arm. She dropped her hand to her side and gave him a whimsical smile. "There I go. With one breath I apologize for being too pushy, and with the next I start pushing all over again. It's a chronic problem of mine, Taylor. What can I say? I'm incurable."

He smiled sweetly, lightly pressing his fingers to her lips. Then, without a word, he turned and started across the street.

"Taylor? What are you going to do?" She heard the note of desperation in her voice but she didn't care.

He kept walking toward his limo, but he glanced back at her. "I'm going to tell Daniel he can head on home and to leave word at home and at the store that I have to be out of town for a few days."

"You mean...you want to leave now? At one o'clock in the morning?"

But Taylor didn't hear her. He was already at the limo, talking to his chauffeur.

The limo pulled out from the curb. Taylor, still standing across the street, turned to look at her, a beguiling smile on his face. "I'm ready to hit the road, if you are."

"I should go upstairs and pack. And what about you? You don't even have . . . a toothbrush."

"We'll stop at an all-night store and pick up whatever stuff we need."

Ali started to say it was crazy to take off like this on the spur of the moment. But it was precisely because it was crazy that she didn't say a word.

TAYLOR HADN'T HAD EVEN a sip of champagne at the art gallery, but he felt positively giddy as he and Ali picked up an assortment of supplies at a nearby twenty-four-hour convenience store—everything from toothbrushes to running shorts.

"Hey, how about this?" Taylor asked, holding up a T-shirt with a grizzly bear emblazoned on the front beneath which was the line, I Can't Bear To Be Without You.

Ali read the tag line, then said, "I don't think red's your color."

He grinned, plucking a duplicate in black from the pile of folded shirts. "To match my bikinis."

Ali actually flushed.

ALI COULD FEEL THE regrets mounting with each mile. What had she been thinking of? Inviting him to her secluded cottage. The two of them alone for days. Why, she didn't even have two bedrooms. He'd have to sleep on the lumpy living room sofa. Or she would. Or neither of them would. . . .

SHE SNUCK A GLANCE at Taylor as she drove along a winding mountain road. He was dozing. Maybe she should just turn around, drive back to Denver and deposit him at his front door. *Because, let's face it,* she told herself, *turning Taylor Fortune into The Fortune Man just isn't the same as turning Eliza Doolittle into My Fair Lady.* But that was proving not to be the least of her worries. Which really had her worried.

Taylor stirred. "Sorry," he murmured. "I must have fallen asleep. Are we almost there?"

They really were only twenty minutes away, but Ali didn't say that. "Maybe this wasn't such a good idea, Taylor. I . . . I didn't even tell Sara. She'll be concerned about where I've gone."

"You can call her in the morning."

"And you can really just take off from Fortune's like this? You are the head of the company. You must have enormous responsibilities."

"I have good people working for me. They can hold down the fort for a few days. I'm big on delegating. Let's face it, I'm not exactly the managerial type."

They were just coming upon an all-night diner. Ali abruptly swung the car into its parking lot. "How about a cup of coffee?" She already had the door open as she asked the question. She realized she was nervous, playing for time again. For the first time in her career, she felt unsure of herself. She found herself questioning her motives. She wasn't on top of the situation. She had doubts. Oh, not so much about turning Taylor into The Fortune Man. Sure, it would be tough, but when the going got tough, that was when Ali Spencer got going. That was when she pulled out all the stops. That was when she felt capable of anything. No. Her doubts were not about the task at hand. They were about whether it was right to coerce Taylor into playing the game. Oh, sure. She could tell herself he stood to gain as much if not more from it than she did, but deep down she knew that Fortune's was doing fine enough without her turning its CEO into a glamorous man-about-town spokesman.

But that wasn't her only concern. She couldn't sort out her feelings about Taylor. And, what was more disconcerting, she didn't like having feelings about him that needed sorting out.

Taylor had to hurry to catch up with her as she marched across the lot studded with a few parked trucks to the diner, a dreary one-story cinder-block rectangle lit up inside by fluorescent tubes, outside by an orange neon sign, Cliffview Diner - Diesel Gas—not exactly an inviting menu.

A bell jingled as they stepped inside, the acrid smell of grease and stale coffee assaulting them. Ali headed straight for the nearest green plastic-seated booth, ignoring the lascivious glances of the truckers lined up along the gray-speckled Formica counter. Taylor didn't fail to notice their looks and gave them all a warning glower. None of the truckers were exactly quaking in their boots, but all but one did turn back around. The one that kept right on giving Ali the eye was a hefty, six-foot-plus bruiser whose insolently sexy half smile fit him as well as his tight-fitting T-shirt, well-worn jeans and scuffed cowboy boots.

The solitary waitress, a middle-aged woman with straw blond hair badly in need of a touch-up, was busy changing the filter of the large steel coffee urn. "Be right with ya," she called out.

The cowboy trucker swung his large frame off the stool, grabbing a menu from a metal clip-on holder on the counter. "Take your time, Georgie. I'll look after your customers," he drawled.

Ali, so caught up in her own worries, was oblivious to the drama developing around her until the trucker, menu in hand, leaned over the table so close to her she could smell his acrid, coffee breath.

"Hi, sugar. What'll it be? If you've got a sweet tooth, there's nothing sweeter than Georgie's blueberry pie. Nothing sweeter 'cept for you, that is."

Ali gave the trucker a rueful smile, thinking to herself that she hadn't heard this hokey a come-on in years. But her smile quickly vanished as she saw the look of fury on Taylor's face.

"Two coffees, two pies," Ali said hurriedly, hoping to get rid of the guy before Taylor took it in his head to do something very silly, like defend her honor.

To her dismay, the trucker leaned even closer to her. "Is that all I can get you, beautiful?"

The trucker was blocking her view so she missed seeing Taylor get up. But then he was looming threateningly over the trucker, who was a good three inches taller than him and several inches wider.

"Taylor..." Ali started to caution.

But it was too late. Taylor grabbed hold of the trucker's right shoulder. "I'd like you to apologize to my friend for your rudeness and insolence, and then I'd like you to leave. Not just leave this booth. Leave the diner."

Ali didn't know whether to marvel at Taylor's nerve, or wonder at his stupidity. She was sure that if the trucker had a mind to, he could make mincemeat out of Taylor. She had to do something to avert a catastrophe.

"Look, pal—" she addressed the trucker in what she hoped was a soothing tone "—it's late, and we're all probably tired and irritable. Why don't you—"

"No, Ali," Taylor said with stubborn resolution. "This man isn't going anywhere until he apologizes to you."

"Taylor..."

The trucker was now eyeing Taylor's hand, which was still gripping his shoulder. He shook his head ruefully. "You're wrinkling the merchandise, buddy. Nothin' gets my goat more than wrinkles, know what I mean?"

"Then I suggest you make your apologies and get out of here," Taylor replied with a laconic calm that amazed and alarmed Ali.

She started to rise. "I really don't want anything. Let's just go, Taylor." There was a pleading note in her voice.

"Sit down, Ali," Taylor said firmly. "There's no reason we have to leave. This gentleman will be leaving. Just as soon as he apologizes."

They were drawing the attention of the rest of the customers and the waitress, who shook her head as if she could already see Taylor sprawled out cold on the dingy yellowed-tile floor. She wore the look of a woman who'd seen that sort of thing many times in the past.

"Please, Taylor," Ali pleaded in earnest, now. "I really want to go."

"The lady wants to go," the trucker echoed with a sarcastic smirk. "The lady can go if she wants to, but you, buddy boy, aren't going anywhere," he drawled, straightening. Taylor's hand slipped away from the trucker's shoulder, but he stood his ground.

"I assume this means you refuse to apologize," Taylor said.

"Look, mister," Ali cut in, "we don't want any trouble. Just chalk this up to my friend's overzealousness." Too late, she realized the trucker probably didn't know the meaning of the word. Or care.

As the trucker turned menacingly around to face the resolute Taylor, Ali could hear a ripple of snickers from the peanut gallery over at the counter. She doubted any of them would come to Taylor's defense. And he was certainly going to need defending. Her gaze fell on the glass sugar dispenser. Allergic as she was to violence of any sort, she seriously entertained the idea of smashing the dispenser over the trucker's head, grabbing Taylor's hand and racing the hell out of there for dear life.

The trucker was eyeballing Taylor. "You want me to apologize, you'll have to make me."

Ali's hand went for the sugar dispenser just as she heard Taylor say with remarkable composure, "If that's the way you want it."

The trucker was already raising his clenched hand toward Taylor's solar plexus as she was lifting the dispenser, ready to clobber him before his punch landed, when the next thing Ali knew, the trucker was letting out a groan that was a mix of shock and pain. A moment later, he fell straight back, landing with a resounding thud onto the floor.

Incredulous, Ali stared down at the splayed trucker and then gazed up in amazement at Taylor, who had just KO'd the guy with a clean right to the jaw.

"How did you . . . do that?" she stammered.

"I boxed in college. Didn't I tell you?" he said offhandedly, removing the sugar dispenser from her hand and setting it back down on the table.

"Was that before or after you took up the bagpipes?" she asked, stunned by the unlikely outcome.

Surprisingly, Taylor, whom the other customers in the diner had clearly taken for the underdog, received a cheerful round of applause. Even the waitress looked pleased to see the trucker get his comeuppance. The only one who didn't look happy was the trucker himself, who was now sitting up, nursing a very painful jaw. Before he got to his feet and made his hasty exit, he did mumble an apology to Ali.

After the trucker left, the waitress brought over two cups of freshly brewed coffee and two slices of apple pie, which she told them, in her opinion, was a lot better than the blueberry pie. And, she added, giving Taylor a flirtatious smile, the "grub" was on the house.

6

THAT PUNCH TAYLOR THREW might not have landed on Ali's jaw, but it knocked some sense into her, anyway.

"Taylor, I think we should go back to Denver."

He pushed aside his plate. "Go back? Now?"

"Yes. Yes, I really think we should."

"You're upset because I punched that fellow out, aren't you? Really, Ali, I'm not a violent man," Taylor said earnestly. "I mean, I've never taken a swing at a guy except in a ring. And that was back in college over ten years ago. I guess I did lose control before. But he had no right speaking to you like that. It was downright disrespectful. I just couldn't . . . allow it."

"Oh, Taylor—' she sighed "—I'm not upset. I'm . . . flattered. I'm more than flattered. I'm . . . touched." She slid her hand across the table, placing it over his hand. "My very own Sir Galahad. And here, all this time, I thought your sort went out with the Round Table."

Taylor looked down at Ali's hand resting over his, then at her face. "Then why do you want to go back to Denver?"

She took a deep breath. "Because I had an ulterior motive for luring you up here."

He smiled. "You did?"

Ali felt her cheeks heat up. "Not that kind of ulterior motive," she mumbled, then pressed her forehead into the palm of her hand. "What I'm trying to say, Taylor, is that I was willing to go to any lengths—almost any lengths—not to lose this deal. Making you into The Fortune Man would give me the kind of notoriety and cash I need to finally open up my own place, be my own boss. I've been incredibly selfish and inconsiderate. You've tried and tried to get out of the deal because it isn't right for you. And what do I do? I keep fast-talking you back in. But it isn't you I'm really thinking about here, Taylor. It's me."

Taylor opened his mouth to speak, but Ali stopped him. "And don't turn it around. Don't make me out to be better than I am. Don't say I'm...assertive. It's selfish, pure and simple." Slowly, she lifted her head. "You're a terrific guy, Taylor. Just the way you are. You're sweet, sincere, protective, tender. What I'm saying here is that you...mean something to me, Taylor, and that wasn't in the cards."

He smiled at her.

But Ali didn't smile back. She didn't want him to mean something to her. She was already sorry she'd let that part slip out. *Better cut to the chase*, she cautioned herself. "I know I'm going to regret this in the morning, but I quit, Taylor. I'm letting you off the hook. Run while you've got the chance. Because I'm wily, Taylor. Give me some time to think about it and I'll start conniving, cajoling, pushing...."

Taylor rose abruptly. "Let's go." His expression was unreadable.

Ali swallowed hard and nodded.

As soon as they stepped foot outside the diner, she was astonished to find herself in Taylor's arms. And then he was kissing her. The kiss wasn't gentle. It was openmouthed and hungry. Sheer surprise made her resist for a moment, but then she was kissing him back, matching his intensity.

When he released her, she gave him a dazed look. "What...was that...for?"

Taylor, more than a little shocked by his impulsive action, but nonetheless pleased, smiled unabashedly. "Ali Spencer, your eyes are like arrows that pierce my heart. Your smile is like the sun warming me. And your touch is like a moon-beam of radiance that reaches into my soul."

His smile faded. "Ali, I've never been the sort of man who went in for romantic conquests or poetic outbursts. I haven't had hordes of women streaming in and out of my bedroom over the years."

He smiled boyishly. "I'm thirty-two years old and I find myself having my first real crush. To be perfectly honest, I'm scared to death that on top of all my other displays of ineptitude and clumsiness, I'll make a mess of this, too. But it doesn't change the reality that I haven't been able to stop thinking about you or longing for you since that first day you burst into my office."

He stopped a moment for breath, but his eyes never left her face. "What I'm trying to say is that I'm about as far from being The Fortune Man as a man can be, but fortune is smiling down on me. And that fortune is you, Ali Spencer."

Ali was overcome. For a woman who thought she was reasonably experienced in the romance department, she was taken for a loop by Taylor's unique, romantic and heartfelt speech. Tears spilled from her eyes. "Oh, Taylor," she murmured. "Now you've gone and done it."

He smoothed back her curls, offering a smile that was surprisingly seductive. Surprising as much to Taylor as to Ali. "Does that mean we won't be going back to Denver tonight?"

ALI FUMBLED IN HER BAG for the key to her cottage. "I know it's here somewhere." She started pulling items out—her wallet, checkbook, compact—tucking them under her chin as her search intensified. Maybe she didn't have her key and they'd have to turn around and go back to Denver, after all. Maybe that would be the smartest move she could make. Certainly, lately, her moves had been anything but.

Taylor gently eased the bag from Ali's grasp and looked her straight in the eye. "Are you nervous?"

"Nervous? No. Why should I be?" Her wallet, checkbook and compact slipped from beneath her chin as she spoke, and fell to the ground. She peered down but it was too dark to see where the items had landed. She could barely make Taylor out in the hazy glimmer of light provided by the sliver of moon. She started to bend down to search out her belongings, but Taylor gripped her arm, stopping her mid-bend.

"I'm nervous, too, Ali," he said with a knowing smile.

She heard a jingle. Taylor had found the key on its ring in her bag. So much for retreat.

He unlocked the front door. Ali reached in and flicked on the small outside light. Taylor picked up the things she'd dropped and dumped them back into her bag. When he rose he realized he was a little dizzy. "Nervous" had been an understatement. He felt like a teenager on his first date. The feeling wasn't all that far from reality.

"Are you coming inside?" Ali asked hesitantly, already having entered the cottage.

Taylor cleared his throat and stepped over the threshold.

"You can put my pocketbook on the table. Unless you'd rather hold on to it," she teased lightly, hoping to break the tension.

Taylor smiled awkwardly and set her bag down. The front door was still open and he went to close it.

"Wait. We forgot the stuff we bought in the convenience store." She started to move past him for the door. Again he caught hold of her. It was hard to tell who was trembling more.

Taylor smiled crookedly. "We could think of this as comic relief."

She pressed her finger to his lips and slowly shook her head.

Taylor kicked the door shut with his foot, shutting out the light. Shutting out the world.

When he kissed her this time, he did it slowly, letting her know that he was moved not simply by lust but by a desire to connect with her, to seek out her true essence, to become a part of her. Ali closed her eyes and gave herself up willingly to his explorations, her fingers threading into his hair as he drew her closer.

The next thing she knew she was being lifted into his arms, her shoes falling off, making a faint thud as they landed. Forget Professor Higgins and Eliza Doolittle—she felt like Scarlett O'Hara in the arms of Rhett Butler.

Until Taylor took five steps in the dark and tripped on the Navaho scatter rug. He did valiantly try to cushion her fall as they went down.

"Are you hurt?" Taylor asked anxiously, mortified by his clumsiness.

Ali laughed softly. "No, Taylor. How about you?"

"Only my pride," he muttered morosely. "I knew something like this would happen."

Ali reached out for him, circling her arms around his neck in the darkness as they sat on the floor. "You were right. I am nervous, Taylor."

There was a long silence and it was so dark in the curtained room Ali couldn't even make out Taylor's features. "Maybe I should shed a little light—" she started to say, only to find her words cut off by Taylor's lips. Her senses began to swim as she lost herself in his kiss.

When she caught her breath afterward, she murmured, "You don't kiss like a guy who's nervous."

He laughed softly. "I don't feel as nervous now. How about you? How do you feel?"

"I'm not . . . sure," she admitted. "I feel a little . . . light-headed."

He bent his head toward hers. He kissed her cheeks, her eyelids, her throat, then lower still, trailing his lips lightly over the silk fabric of her dress. Her nipples were already hard and her pulse was fluttering wildly.

"I know how you feel. You feel incredible," he whispered against her breast, his warm breath seeping right through the thin cloth, heating her skin.

She found herself curled around him on the woven Navaho rug. Taylor's hands were splayed across her back as he held her close. They were less than twenty steps from her bedroom and its big, inviting double bed, but Ali didn't want to move. She had never felt so completely held, so completely content in a man's embrace.

Putting one hand alongside her cheek to guide her face, he once again put his mouth on hers. His kiss was soft, firm, tender, insistent all at once. Ali felt a little jolt in her heart. And a rush of nervous anticipation. What Taylor lacked in experience he was more than making up for in ingenuity and incredible tenderness.

"Taylor?"

"Yes, Ali?"

"You know this is going to change everything. I mean, our relationship will . . . be different. That's why I've always had this rule about not mixing business with pleasure."

He slowly lowered the zipper that ran down the back of her dress. "Lift your arms, Ali."

She did as he asked without protest, but kept on talking. "I don't want you to think I make a practice of this sort of thing with clients. Even reluctant clients. Any clients. Ever. I never have. When I said before that I would go to almost any lengths, I didn't mean . . . I mean, I never have before. With a client. . . ."

He slipped her dress over her head. "Your client is The Fortune Man. I'm not him. Yet, anyway. I hardly know him."

Ali felt a cool breeze on her bare skin. "You hardly know me, too."

"You, I want to get to know better," he murmured, releasing the catch of her bra.

Instinctively, Ali's hands went to cover her breasts as the bra fell to the floor. What was she doing? Taylor was slipping her panties off now. In a moment she would be stark naked. Suddenly, she was awash in panic. Every one of her emotions had been switched to high. Her lust made her embarrassed. How had she allowed herself to get into such a state?

"Roll over." Taylor's voice was a gentle whisper, but she obeyed his command as if he were her drill sergeant.

Still dressed, he straddled her and gently but firmly went to work on the knotted muscles radiating down her back and across her shoulders. He kneaded gently, a low moan of pleasure escaping Ali's lips. Slowly, Taylor felt the muscles become resilient again, releasing their tension.

"Oh, Taylor, you have magic fingers," Ali whispered. And even in that moment of sublime pleasure she couldn't help thinking that here was a talent of Taylor's that she wished she could capitalize on for her campaign. The Fortune Man's magic fingers. . . .

But as Taylor continued working his magic down, down, down her spine, all thought evaporated and she glided into a realm of pure sensation.

"That feels so wonderful, Taylor."

He leaned low, pressing his mouth to her ear. "Comes from playing the bagpipes."

They both laughed quietly. But the laughter faded as Taylor's ministrations took on a new, more sensual quality.

"Your skin feels smoother than silk," he said, drawing in a breath, savoring the scent and softness of her skin, luxuriating in the warmth radiating from both their bodies, their heat already mingling.

Ali's fever-pitch arousal didn't allow for leisurely helping Taylor out of his clothes. She went about the task with a vengeance, literally popping several buttons off his shirt— and jamming the zipper of his fly. They both giggled and yanked until the zipper broke altogether. Okay. So in this department, anyway, she lacked Taylor's natural artistry. What could she do? She was burning with impatience and desire to feel the naked length of him against her. They flung his clothes across the room. And when, at last, her wish came true and she felt the warmth of his skin pressed against hers, she felt as if she was drowning in a rich, romantic sensuality.

Ali was ready, willing, and more than eager, but Taylor rolled off her. "I want to see you," he murmured. "Put on a light."

Ali hesitated. In the darkness, it all felt somehow unreal, a fantasy. Somehow, in the darkness, she imagined she could deny responsibility for her lust.

He took hold of her hand, held it tightly, caressing the back of it with his thumb. "Please, Ali."

A tremor chased over her shoulders. She could get up, and instead of switching on the light, grab up her clothes and make a run for it. Because, damn it all, in the light she'd have to acknowledge what she was doing and he'd see how much she wanted to be doing what she was doing. And she'd see how much he wanted it. You couldn't hide in the light. You couldn't hold on to any pretense.

She did get up, but she didn't run. She flicked on a nearby lamp and stood in its glow, like a scared, disoriented rabbit suddenly caught in the high beams of a car's headlights. Taylor sat up and stared at her, his gaze steady and very serious. And, Ali thought, frustratingly composed for a man who had less than an hour ago confessed that he was anything but a

Don Juan. How ironic that here she stood, the supposedly assured woman of the world, shivering like a virgin schoolgirl, licking her dry lips while her heart hammered in her chest and her pulse fluttered in her throat.

"Say something," she pleaded, her attempt at a smile falling short.

"Come here."

She came toward him, her legs wobbly, her head spinning.

He stood. She stopped several feet from him. "You're beautiful," she said in awe as she took in his firm, sleek, slender body with its fine musculature.

He smiled at her. "That's my line. Only it isn't a line. I couldn't hand you a line if I wanted to. And I don't want to. You're a vision, Ali. It's like having a fantasy come true before my eyes. Beyond my wildest dreams. I'm a little scared that if I touch you now, you'll evaporate into thin air."

"Touch me, Taylor." She stepped closer, amazed to discover it was better in the light. There was such tenderness in Taylor's features, such exquisite grace in his body. Surely this couldn't be the same man who had stepped on her toes dancing, accidentally dislodged a piece of sculpture, got caught in a battle with his robot in an elevator. . . .

He was enfolding her in his arms, his lips on hers. He kissed her softly, lingeringly, provocatively. She didn't evaporate, but the whole time he was kissing her, reveling in her firm, shapely body, twining his fingers around her impossible curls, he was telling himself this was a dream. He had to be dreaming. . . .

They discovered they were standing right by a large, antique, gilt-framed mirror. They both gazed at their reflection in the glass. There was something incredibly erotic about seeing their naked selves entwined in each other's arms. Slowly, Taylor pivoted her around to face the mirror as he moved behind her, his hands reaching for her breasts, cupping their fullness in his palms. As her eyes fixed on the mirror, a vortex of emotions coursed through her. Her legs went weak and she leaned hard against him, her gaze never shifting.

He, too, watched her reflection in the glass as he stroked and fondled her breasts, circling her hard nipples that were the color of pale pink tea roses, capturing them between his fingers, kneading them. Then one of his hands drifted lower, down over the curve of her waist, slowly, sinuously moving over her flat belly to the auburn leaf of hair so startlingly explicit between her creamy hips. Finally his fingers—his magic fingers—dipped lower still.

Ali had never before actually witnessed herself in the throes of passion. It seemed to double the intensity. No, more than double it, because it took on extra power seeing Taylor watching, too—watching her with such tenderness, lust, and fascination, and watching himself touch and stroke and caress her.

"Oh, God, Taylor . . ." she murmured weakly, her breath ragged. "I'm going to—" The words were cut off by a deep, guttural moan, her whole body shimmering in spasm as her eyes fluttered closed in that last instant and she collapsed against him.

Gently, he lifted her up in his arms again. This time he didn't trip as he carried her through the open door into the bedroom. The lamplight from the living room bathed the bedroom in a soft, romantic glow. Carefully, as if she were a fragile jewel, he eased her down on the inviting white chenille spread covering the double bed. But her arms, which were twined around his neck, pulled him down heavily upon her, convincing him she was far less fragile than he'd thought.

"I'll crush you."

Her eyes fluttered open and she smiled provocatively
"Please."

Even in his piercing, burning desire to possess her fully, he
held back. "There's one thing we didn't get at that conve
nience store," he murmured.

Ali gave him a fuzzy look and then the light dawned. "Oh.
But then she smiled. "I'm on the Pill."

"You are?" As much as he was relieved, he was also dis
appointed.

Her smile deepened as she stroked his cheek. "I haven'
been with another man in a long time, Taylor. I'm on the Pi
to help regulate my period."

He cupped her face and kissed her with joyous abandor
Ali arched into him, draping her slender legs around him
feeling his lust, making it her own. As his hands began t
move down her body in a possessive yet tender way, her hip
began to undulate of their own accord.

His hand snaked between their bodies, molding he
breasts. "Does this feel good, Ali?"

"Yes," she gasped.

Tantalizingly, lifting above her, he eased himself just barel
inside her. "And this?"

For answer, her mouth pressed hard against his for a deep
probing, delirious kiss.

They were both trembling. As Ali's hands moved ove
Taylor's strong, lean body, he entered her fully in one dee
thrust that made her breath catch in her throat. Their eye
were open. Now they were each the mirror for the othe
aware of each other with every one of their senses. All of th
emotion within them played on their faces. And for each
was a richness of discovery.

"Oh, Taylor," she gasped, "this feels so good. I neve
dreamed it could be so good."

Their hungry mouths met, their eyes closed and she lifted her hips to his thrusting body, pliant and yielding and for the first time in her life holding nothing back, allowing him not only to enter her body but to touch her in a far more intimate way.

When release came, she cried out with unabashed abandon. A moment later, she heard him whisper her name—a whisper swallowed up in his own low cry of deliverance.

He rolled off her, as if still not convinced his weight wouldn't crush her. "I feel so good, Ali." He lay on his side facing her, studying her appreciatively.

She faced him, too, and smiled. "You were wonderful."

He smiled back. "And that surprises you."

"Yes," she admitted. But, after a pause, she added, "I suppose it shouldn't have. You do everything with such openness and honesty. Why not lovemaking?" Her smile evaporated and she closed her eyes. "I'm not used to this. I'm feeling . . ."

"Tell me," he coaxed softly when she didn't finish.

He waited. He could almost feel her struggle. They'd made love, but he sensed that for her there were greater risks.

"I told you...before...that our relationship would change, Taylor. But I don't honestly know what that change is going to be. I'm not sure what I want it to be. And I hate not being sure of things." She rolled away from him. "I know this is going to sound really stupid, but I think we ought to . . . keep this in perspective, Taylor. Okay, so we went to bed. And it was great. It was great, Taylor. But I don't want you to . . . to get carried away. Because I'm not going to get carried away. You need to know that."

"You don't have to always be so tough, so sure of yourself, Ali," he replied, curving himself spoon-fashion around her. "That's it, isn't it? You're scared. You're more scared than cynical."

She craned her neck and eyed him cautiously. "How do you know so much?"

He merely smiled.

Ali felt her defenses resurface. "I am cynical. I have plenty of reasons to be. I watched my parents split up, and then I watched them both split from their new spouses. I've got two sisters—one struggling to make a go of her second marriage, the other a three-time loser. I don't have what you'd call great role models where marriage is concerned. I think it's just too hard for most people. Especially if you have a career. I always figured I was better off making it on my own. It's worked okay for me so far." She sighed. "What I'm trying to say, Taylor, is that I never let myself get too involved. That's my credo. I never let things go too far."

"What's too far?"

She gave him a wry smile. "Well, at least I know you aren't going to spring a marriage proposal on me, Taylor. Or else I might really be scared."

WHEN TAYLOR AWOKE, early the next morning, he wasn't surprised to discover Ali had gone. Because he knew she was scared, of course. There was a note resting on her pillow. She'd taken the car back to Denver and arranged for his chauffeur, Daniel, to pick him up at the cottage at ten o'clock.

Despite Ali's vanishing act, Taylor remained in a buoyant mood. At precisely ten on the button Daniel knocked on the cottage door. Taylor, whose clothing from last evening was unwearable, appeared at the door dressed in a pair of cheap white shorts and the black T-shirt with the bear plastered on the front. He greeted his chauffeur with a bright smile.

Daniel, who prided himself on always maintaining proper decorum and discretion as befitted his post, couldn't hide his expression of surprise at Taylor's appearance and demeanor. And his eyebrow arched of its own accord as he read the motto beneath the bear: I Can't Bear To Be Without You.

Taylor grinned. And then to add to Daniel's surprise, his employer slung an affable arm around his shoulders. "Daniel," Taylor said, "how about giving me a driving lesson."

"HE DID WHAT?" Peter exclaimed.

"He drove the limo home," Adam repeated slowly, as if he were addressing a not-quite-bright child.

"But he can't drive," Peter argued.

"Daniel said the same thing," Adam said dryly.

"Home from where?" Tru demanded.

Adam sank down on the sofa in his living room. "Ali Spencer's little retreat about an hour north of here."

Peter sat down beside him. "Her...retreat? Are you sure?"

Adam gave him a sideways glance and nodded.

Tru sat down across from Adam. "Maybe she let him use the place. Maybe he wanted to be away from town, away from the store, away from the hassles. He probably wanted to work on some design changes for Homer. Or for one of his other gadgets."

Adam waited patiently for Tru to finish. "He wasn't alone."

Tru and Peter shared sinking looks.

"Ali . . ." Peter said.

"And Taylor . . . ?" Tru added.

Adam nodded.

"They didn't . . . ?" Peter whispered.

Again Adam nodded.

"Oh, come on. Taylor? Romancing a woman like Ali Spencer into bed?" Peter said incredulously. "How do you know?"

Tru looked at Adam. "He confided in Eve?"

Adam shook his head.

"He told you?" Peter queried.

"He told Gran," Adam answered solemnly.

"Gran," Peter repeated despairingly.

"Oh, great. Talk about throwing a little fuel on the fire," Tru muttered acerbically.

Peter sighed. "I suppose he thinks he's in love with her."

Adam arched a brow. "We're talking about Taylor here, remember? Of course he thinks he's in love with her."

Tru slammed his palm down on the cherrywood coffee table. "But she's just playing him for a sap. I know her type. She's got the account of a lifetime riding on this. And she was probably worried Taylor might have second thoughts about this crazy Fortune Man nonsense."

"I know for a fact," Adam broke in, "that Taylor was having second thoughts. He told Eve he just didn't see how he could ever be the kind of suave, assured man-about-town that Ali envisioned. For all we know, Taylor might have told Ali he wanted out of the deal. What would a woman like Ali Spencer do in that situation, seeing the deal of a lifetime slip through her fingers? I'll tell you what she'd do. She'd seduce Taylor, knowing he was bound to fall head over heels in love with her. And then she'd have him just where she wanted him."

Peter scowled. "No, I know Ali. That's not her style. I grant you, she can be pretty ruthless and cutthroat, but she doesn't play dirty. I can't believe she would have—"

"Compromised our baby brother?" Tru finished ruefully. "I suppose next thing you're going to tell me, Pete, is that she's gaga over him, too. But I'll lay you odds the lady doesn't have marriage on her mind. Because if she gets Taylor down that aisle, she can kiss The Fortune Man goodbye. And we all know The Fortune Man is her ticket to fame and fortune, brothers. And that's what she's after—not love and marriage to a poor but endearing inventor, which is what Taylor would end up being the moment he said, 'I do.'"

Adam shot up from the couch. "I think we ought to pay Ms. Ali Spencer a little visit. Have it out with her. Find out exactly what her intentions are, regarding our baby brother."

"You're right," Tru said. "We have to look out for Taylor. Let's face it, when it comes to matters of the heart he's just an innocent babe in the woods."

Peter rubbed his jaw. "We really do owe it to Taylor to nip this thing in the bud. Otherwise the poor guy's going to wind up with a broken heart."

"Whereas," Tru continued philosophically, "if we get her to show her true colors before he gets too carried away, he'll wind up thanking us in the end."

"Unless we're wrong about her," Adam said slowly. "Unless Taylor does mean more to her than a ticket to fame and fortune."

Adam hesitated. "As unlikely as we all seem to think it is, there is that small possibility she *is* gaga over him."

The three brothers stared at each other, all realizing the import of those words. What they meant were "Goodbye Fortune's, hello Fielding's." Why wouldn't Nolan Fielding change the name, once he was the sole owner of the Fortune empire?

There was a silence.

"Okay," Peter said finally. "Let's admit it. There's more on the line here than Taylor's love life."

"ALI SPENCER, WILL YOU please tell me what's going on?"

Ali brushed past Sara with her suitcase, which she'd retrieved from the shelf of her closet.

"Nothing's going on," Ali muttered, flipping open the lid and hurrying over to her bureau where she proceeded to grab clothes at random and gather them in her arms. "I have to go out of town on business."

"Where were you until seven this morning?" Sara queried, giving her roommate and friend a scrutinizing look.

Ali scowled as she crossed back to the bed and began dumping her clothes into the suitcase in a less-than-orderly fashion. She might have been a prison escapee on the lam. "Really, Sara, you sound like my mother." Her scowl deepened. "Well, maybe not *my* mother, but somebody's mother."

Sara merely smiled. "Sometimes you need mothering, Ali. Maybe if you'd had more of it, you wouldn't be racing out of the house like a scared rabbit."

"I told you, I've got to go out of town on business."

"And does that business have anything to do with your Fortune Man campaign?" Sara persisted despite the mounting hostility in Ali's tone.

Ali slammed the lid of her suitcase shut. "There is no Fortune Man campaign. I must have been completely out of my mind to think that I could turn a man who is so green, so unsophisticated, so . . . damn naive into . . . into a slick, debonair . . ."

"Cad?" Sara offered with a facetious smile.

Ali glared at her, but Sara didn't stop smiling, although the smile did soften and become more sympathetic. It was the sympathy that got to Ali. She sank down on the bed beside her suitcase.

"I think the big jerk's in love with me," she muttered.

"Big jerk? He must have gotten to you," Sara teased, but she looked even more sympathetic now.

Ali scrunched her eyes shut for a moment so as to still the tears. When she opened her eyes they came anyway. "I always thought I was so clever, so shrewd, so smart. I had everything mapped out and I was nothing if not an ace navigator."

Sara sat down beside Ali. "And last night you steered off course?"

"Off course, nothing. I steered myself right into a typhoon." Ali stared wistfully at her roommate. "Oh, but what a ride it was while it lasted, Sara."

"It doesn't look to me like it's over."

The wistful look vanished. In its place came sheer determination. "It's got to be over. I can't handle it. There, I'm admitting it. I met my Waterloo and his name is Taylor Fortune."

Having made her confession, she grabbed up her suitcase and started for the door.

Sara rushed after her, catching hold of her sleeve. "You didn't tell me where you're going. Or for how long?"

Ali swatted away her tears with her free hand. "I'm going to New York. For a couple of weeks, anyway. Maybe... longer. Until I can get my life back on course."

7

EVE FORTUNE HAD TO SIT a little farther back from the table to accommodate what her husband, Adam, playfully called her "kangaroo pouch." Seven months pregnant and she already felt as large as a house. And as happy as a lark. At least, she'd been happy until about five minutes ago when Taylor Fortune, who sat across from her in a small café in downtown Denver, began delivering his heartfelt plea for help.

When he'd finished, she tried to think of something reasonable, objective, and gently discouraging to say. However, nothing like that came into her head. Instead, she merely asked, "Are you sure about this, Taylor?"

Taylor set aside his club sandwich. "Absolutely sure, Eve," he replied without hesitation. "I've already made a little progress with Ali. Although I will admit she got discouraged."

"But you didn't?" Eve couldn't help asking.

"Oh, I did," Taylor admitted. "I was ready to call it quits on any number of occasions. But when it gets down to the bottom line, I'm just not a quitter, Eve. You can't be an inventor and get easily discouraged. There's always so much trial and error."

"But we're not talking about being an inventor now, Taylor," Eve reminded him.

Taylor smiled sheepishly. "No. I know we're not, Eve. We're talking about a guy who's the complete opposite of an inventor. We're talking about a guy who knows all the right moves and when to make them, a guy who says all the right things at the right times, a guy who's charming, sexy, charismatic." His smile turned into a grin. "In short, we're talking here about The Fortune Man."

Eve nodded slowly, not sure what to say.

Taylor leaned forward, elbows on the table. Well, actually, one elbow landed in his side dish of coleslaw, but Eve pretended not to notice.

"When Ali gets back from her business trip in New York I want to be able to convince her that I have what it takes to be The Fortune Man," Taylor said earnestly, after which he noticed where his elbow had landed. He quickly lifted his arm and Eve, already in a maternal mode, picked up her napkin, took hold of his arm, and wiped the mess off his sleeve.

Taylor laughed. "I'm sure The Fortune Man would know better than to put his elbows on the table in the first place," he said, placing his hands on the table now. "So, what do you think, Eve?"

"It's a tall order," she admitted. "How much time . . . ?"

"Her roommate, Sara, thinks she'll be gone for a couple of weeks, anyway. I can take some time off and devote myself fully to the task. I figure with your help, Gran's, and Elizabeth and Sasha pitching in, I should be able to make a fair amount of progress."

Eve wasn't so sure. There was also something else on her mind. "Taylor, you know how your brothers feel about you getting too involved with Ali Spencer. They're all terrified that you're going to wind up falling head over heels in love with her and asking her to marry you. Let's face it, none of them want to see Fortune's turned over to an outsider. Even though Nolan Fielding seems like a very nice man. . . ."

"He *is* a very nice man, Eve, but he isn't going to be running Fortune's. I am," Taylor said emphatically. "I have no intention of getting married."

"Neither did Adam, Pete, or Tru, if you recall," Eve reminded with a wry smile.

"That was different. Or I should say, Ali and I are different. Let's face it, there would be no Fortune Man if I got hitched—to Ali or anyone else. I'm doing all of this in order to put Fortune's on the map. Just think, Eve, no one—not Adam, Tru or Peter—thought I'd make a go of running Fortune's. Don't you see? This is my chance to prove them all wrong."

"You're sure you're only out to prove something to *them?*" Eve asked.

"You mean Ali?" He smiled sheepishly. "Okay, maybe I want to prove something to her, too."

"You could be treading on dangerous ground, Taylor."

"Look, Eve. Ali and I are not going to get . . . too entangled. Neither of us wants that. She knows marriage is out for me. And as for her, she would probably rather walk over burning coals than walk down the aisle. So what's the danger? All I want to do is market my inventions—especially Homer—and make the company more successful than it has ever been. And I really believe Ali's come up with the perfect way for me to achieve that goal. I want to prove to her I can carry it off before she throws in the towel. Now, will you help me or won't you?"

Eve squeezed his hand affectionately. "I guess my problem is I think you're wonderful just the way you are."

"Come on, Eve. At the moment, I've got two left feet, I can't for the life of me figure out if you wear stripes with plaids or if that's totally de rigueur, I'm lousy at light, flirtatious chitchat, I'm a menace behind a wheel, I don't know Puccini from Gucci. . . ."

Eve laughed. "Okay, okay, I get the point. You'd better stop before I really start getting discouraged."

"Then you will . . . ?"

Eve frowned. "You know your brothers would have a bird if they knew we were helping you. They'd think we were conspiring—"

"To help me make Fortune's bigger than ever," he hastily finished for her.

"It's obvious you're attracted to her."

"Sure, I'm attracted to her," Taylor admitted. "She's beautiful, she's got a great figure, she's dynamic, independent, self-confident. But let's face it, I'm not exactly her type."

"But The Fortune Man might be," Eve said with a faint smile.

"Does that mean you'll help me?"

Eve hesitated. She was torn. Despite what Taylor claimed were his motives for wanting to be The Fortune Man, Eve was quite certain he was already smitten with Ali and that somewhere in the back of his mind was the hope that she would fall for The Fortune Man. And what if he was right? Eve was all for love—even marriage, if in the end that was Taylor's and Ali's choice—but she was concerned about Taylor feeling he had to make himself over in order to win Ali's affections.

But then Eve smiled. Hadn't she done just that to prove to Adam that he was really in love with her?

Taylor was watching her intently. When he saw her smile, he knew she would help him. He reached across and squeezed her arm, accidentally knocking over her glass of lemonade in the process. He apologized profusely as the waitress came over and sopped up the puddle of liquid and ice cubes from the table and from Eve's lap. "You see how much help I need. I get flustered, clumsy, awkward, especially when I get nervous or . . . excited," he said and flushed.

"It's not going to be a snap, Taylor. You'll need dance lessons. . . ." She grinned, patting her stomach. "I'll leave that to Elizabeth. And Sasha's the one to give you the driving lessons. Although you might also want to take a course at a driving school. As for clothes, I can help you there. And so can Jessica. And we'll all pitch in to give you some lessons on being suave and debonair. Are you sure you're ready for this, Taylor?"

He smiled ingenuously. "I'll work day and night."

"THAT'S IT, TAYLOR," Elizabeth said encouragingly. "Now dip me. Lower. A little lower. A little more...."

"Oops. Sorry, Elizabeth."

She grinned. "That was just a smidgen too low," she said as he helped her rise from the floor. "But, other than that, I'd say you've got the fox-trot down. Want to take a breather?"

"No. I mean, not unless you—"

"Me? I could dance all night," she said with a laugh.

"Good," Taylor said eagerly. "Then let's work on the samba again. And then the cha-cha. There's one tricky step there...."

AT TEN O'CLOCK IN THE morning Taylor sat nervously behind his brand-new red Ferrari convertible for his first lesson.

"Okay, turn on the ignition and pump the gas pedal," Sasha instructed.

Taylor shot her a teasing look. "That's the one on the far right, right?"

"Right," Sasha said solemnly.

After several false starts, Sasha told him to use the choke. Taylor promptly turned on the radio.

By two that afternoon, however, Taylor was beginning to get the hang of it. They were moving at a reasonable clip along a winding two-lane road, when Taylor noticed a truck rapidly moving up on him from behind. He got a little nervous and slowed down to let the truck pass. But they were coming to a sharp S-turn and it was too dangerous for the truck to make the maneuver.

"Give it gas, Taylor. The worst thing is to be indecisive," Sasha said firmly, regarding what was happening in her side-view mirror.

"Right," Taylor muttered. "Decisive. Got it." He floored the gas pedal as they came into the curve.

"Well, not so much gas, Taylor," Sasha said hoarsely after the little sports car nearly took the curve on two wheels.

Taylor grinned. "A bit too decisive?"

"LISTEN CAREFULLY TO THIS aria now, Taylor," Jessica instructed her grandson. She started the tape.

Taylor was quiet for a couple of minutes, his expression a study in concentration. He looked over at her. "*La Tosca?*"

"Close," she enthused. "It's by the same composer."

"Don Giovanni?"

"No, dear. *Don Giovanni* is an opera, not a composer. Puccini. Puccini composed *La Tosca*," she repeated, trying not to lose patience.

"Right," Taylor said. "Puccini." He grinned at his grandmother. "You're sure he's no relation to Gucci?"

"Perhaps we should return to Gilbert and Sullivan," Jessica suggested.

"Weren't they the ones who invented the wine cooler, Gran?" Taylor teased.

"NO, TAYLOR," EVE corrected. "I said a *hooded* gaze. Don't actually close your eyes."

"No. You're squinting now," Elizabeth said.

"Like this." Sasha demonstrated.

Everyone laughed. Sasha arched an eyebrow. "Well, that is it, isn't it?"

"Absolutely," Eve replied, speaking for all of them. "Now, you try again, Taylor."

"Wait," Elizabeth said. "Start with your entrance, Taylor. Let's say you're walking into a cocktail party or coming down to the lobby during a concert or opera intermission. Remember, you pause at the door—"

"Or at the next-to-the-bottom step if you're in a concert hall," Elizabeth interrupted.

Eve nodded, picking up where she left off. "Shoulders back, just the slightest tilt of the head, chin up, as you glance around. The faintest smile on your lips—"

"Yes," Sasha broke in. "For a touch of mystery, danger. Oh, yes, I love a man with a mysterious, dangerous aura," she murmured, thinking of Tru.

Taylor tried it. He looked more pained than mysterious, more frightened than dangerous. The women tried not to laugh, but Taylor sensed he wasn't doing it right.

"Think of something wild and reckless," Sasha suggested.

Taylor frowned. "Wild and reckless?"

"Yes. It will show in your face," Eve agreed. "Surely you've had fantasies, Taylor. Especially lately."

Taylor felt his cheeks redden, but he nodded.

"None of us have to know what it is, Taylor," Elizabeth said softly. "Give it a try."

Taylor felt incredibly foolish, but then he remembered that this was all his idea, and his sisters-in-law and grandmother were only trying to help. He closed his eyes. A few moments later, he pictured Ali riding a white steed through the canyons, being chased by a gang of thieves. Then there he was, atop one of the canyons, dressed all in black, on a black steed. He looked down the steep gorge, saw that she was in terrible trouble, and knew that he would risk life and limb to rescue her. He started down—

"Hold it. That's the look!" Eve shouted.

"Bold, daring," Sasha added.

"And damn sexy," Elizabeth murmured, the others all agreeing.

Taylor blushed in earnest, but he was also beaming. "Okay, okay. Let me try it again."

"Only this time, open your eyes," Eve suggested.

"And keep your body nice and loose, Taylor," Elizabeth offered.

"And lift your eyebrow just a fraction," Jessica piped in. "I think that's always a nice touch."

"REMEMBER, TAYLOR, it's not so much what you say, but how you say it," Eve said as they stood around at a mock cocktail party. "And you might go with just the hint of a cowboy drawl."

"Yes, but keep in mind," Elizabeth said, "that actions often speak louder than words."

"I think it is always good to be the strong, silent type," Sasha offered.

"But when you do say something," Eve pointed out, "it should be slightly provocative."

"But not too provocative," Elizabeth warned.

"A bit glib...."

"But not too glib."

"And never use a cliché."

"But don't try to be too original."

"Have an air of detachment—"

"But don't come across disinterested."

"Don't be too eighties."

That one got him. He gave Eve a baffled look. "Too eighties?"

Eve smiled. "You know. Too aggressive, too sure of yourself."

"But he can't be unsure of himself, either," Elizabeth advised.

Sasha nodded. "This is true whether you are American or Russian. You must be confident but not overly confident."

"The Fortune Man has to be a nineties man, Taylor," Eve explained. "Still charming, suave and debonair, but with just the right blend of virtue, sensitivity...."

"Yes, women must trust you...."

"But, of course, not too much, or you'll be viewed as soft."

"Exactly. You must be strong, but not hard."

"All right." Eve eyed Taylor. "Are you ready?"

Taylor hesitated.

"Are you nervous, Taylor?" Elizabeth asked.

He broke into a grin. "Yes, but not too nervous."

"WHY, JESSIE, I'VE NEVER seen you look more radiant," Ben Engel said as he came upon Jessica Fortune, busy pruning marigolds in her garden.

She rose energetically before he could help her to her feet, tipping her head up slightly so that he could give her a peck on the cheek. "Oh, Ben, I have such good news to tell you," she exclaimed, her face even more animated than usual.

"I have some good news of my own," Ben said, taking her hand in his. "But you go first."

They sat down on a circular bench built around a fragrant eucalyptus tree. "It's Taylor. He's in love. He's in love with Ali Spencer. Oh, he doesn't know it fully yet, but it's as plain as the nose on his face. A fine nose, at that." She smiled brightly. "Isn't that wonderful, Ben?"

He tilted his head and smiled at her. But he didn't respond immediately.

Jessica knew Ben well enough at this point to know something was troubling him. "I didn't really have anything to do with it," she hastened to add. "Other than arranging their first meeting, that is," she added with a twinkle in her blue eyes. "After that, to my admitted surprise, Taylor carried the ball."

Ben squeezed Jessica's hand. "Oh, I'm the last one to be chastising you for meddling. After all, didn't I conspire with you to help Elizabeth and Peter realize that they belonged together?"

Jessica smiled. "Yes. And didn't that turn out just wonderfully?"

"Oh, indeed. They make a perfect couple. As do Adam and Eve, and Tru and Sasha. But—"

"But you're not so sure about Taylor and Ali," Jessica surmised.

Ben hesitated. "You say Taylor's in love with Ali, but is she in love with him?"

Jessica's eyes sparkled and she gave him a conspiratorial look. "In a weak moment, Taylor confided to me that they spent a night together, Ben. And the very next day she ran off to New York."

Ben gave her a puzzled look.

Jessica laughed. "Don't you see? She must care for him or she wouldn't have run off."

Ben grinned. "This is a logic I don't pretend to understand, but I have no doubt you're probably right. You seem to have a sixth sense about these things."

"Oh, I am right, Ben. You've got to see Ali as I do. She's this dynamic, independent, tough cookie who has never let herself get sidetracked before. And what happens the minute she does? She runs scared. But she'll be back, Ben. You mark my words. When it's right, eventually you have to face up to it. And it's right for Taylor and Ali."

Ben shrugged. "I still don't see it. It seems to me that they're as different as night and day. Taylor is a delightful and appealing young man, but dynamic, outgoing, aggressive? No. He is the complete opposite of Ali."

Jessica's eyes sparkled and she gave him an impish smile. "For one thing, Taylor is changing. I think next time you see him you'll be quite surprised."

Jessica went on more seriously. "But for another thing, Ben, I believe that when you peel away the veneers from both of them, you'll find two tender, caring, vulnerable people in search of love. Or, I should say, on the very brink of discovering it."

When she finished, he was smiling at her. It was a rather mysterious smile. Even seductive. She felt pleased and flustered at the same time. "You didn't tell me... your good news."

Ben sat up a little straighter, his gaze remaining on her face, his smile remaining, as well. "I've bought a small house here in Denver."

"Why, Ben, that's wonderful. Then I'll—we'll all—be seeing more of you now."

He gently touched her cheek. "I've moved here so I that I can court you properly, Jessica Fortune."

Jessica lowered her eyes demurely. "Ben Engel, I'm an old woman and you make me feel like a blushing schoolgirl."

"To me, you are neither," he said softly, cupping her chin. "To me, you are a beautiful, vibrant jewel of a woman."

Jessica slowly shook her head in wonder. "Is it really true that one is never too old for romance?"

He kissed her chastely on the forehead, but the sparkle in his eyes was anything but chaste. "Never, my dear Jessie."

CLOSE TO TWO WEEKS AFTER Taylor's tête-à-tête with Eve, Taylor joined his brothers at their usual table at the club for lunch. As he approached them, he could feel the tension in the air. Nevertheless, he greeted all three with a bright smile and a warm hello as he slid into his chair, which was wedged between Adam and Peter, facing Tru.

All three brothers gave Taylor long looks, taking note of the newly acquired tan, the smart-looking designer shirt open at the collar to reveal a thick gold chain, the new haircut, the diamond-and-ruby pinkie ring. But it wasn't so much the tangibles about his appearance that were striking, although indeed they were, but the intangibles. There was something different in Taylor's manner, in the way he carried himself. A new confidence, even an allure. They weren't the only ones to notice the changes, either. As Taylor had approached their table, his brothers had observed that a number of women in the club dining room had also sat up and taken notice. One of them, Tru saw, was coming toward their table.

Taylor, unaware of her approach, blithely picked up a menu. "So, what looks good?"

"Other than you?" a sultry voice murmured from behind him. Taylor craned his neck to see a saucy blonde who looked vaguely familiar.

She helped him out. "Jill Barnett. We met at the Marley gallery a couple of weeks ago."

Taylor smiled sheepishly. "Oh, right. How could I forget the Marley gallery?" His smile subtly changed, was now decidedly charming. "Or you, Miss Barnett?" He smiled inwardly, too, thinking how pleased Elizabeth, Sasha, and Eve would have been with his insouciant comeback.

The gossip columnist looked delighted, as well. "Jill, please," she said, her eyes fixed on his. Then, as if realizing she was being rude, she gave a nod to the other Fortune brothers, before immediately refocusing on Taylor. "I won't keep you from your lunch, but I would still love to get together and hear more about that Fortune Man campaign."

Taylor nodded enthusiastically. "Terrific. I'd love to get some press. As long as you won't forget to put a plug in for my publicist, Ali Spencer. After all, this campaign is her baby. She deserves all the credit."

"Oh, I won't forget her. Or you," Jill said, leaning forward and discreetly slipping her business card into Taylor's shirt pocket. "Marvelous shirt. Lauren?"

"Close," he replied with a wink. "Laurent. Yves Saint."

Jill ran her hand lightly across his shoulder. "I'm sure he'd be delighted."

Taylor took the compliment in stride—which was more than could be said for his three brothers, all of whom watched the flirtatious little exchange in amazement.

After Jill sashayed off, Adam gave Taylor a sideways glance. "Since when do you know a Lauren from a Laurent?"

"Since I raided your closet," Taylor said, grinning. "Eve assured me you wouldn't mind."

Tru leaned back in his chair. "What are you trying to do here, Taylor? This isn't you. I'll be straight with you, kid. If some high-powered, high-pressured woman came along and wanted to turn me inside out, change me from tip to toe, I'd show her the door faster than she could say... Yves Saint Laurent."

"Tru's right," Pete joined in. "You're getting carried away, Taylor."

"You're letting your hormones lead you by the nose," Adam added.

Taylor made no reply to any of these comments. Instead he motioned for the waitress, a cute redhead who smiled provocatively at The Fortune Man as she flipped open her order pad.

"What would you like... to eat?" she asked in a Marilyn Monroe voice.

"How's the chicken gumbo?" Taylor asked, his tone a mix of Bogart and Cary Grant.

She actually fluttered her eyelids. "Spicy, but I recommend it."

Taylor smiled at her. "Then how can I resist?" He glanced around the table at his brothers, all of whom were gaping at him in sheer astonishment. "What do you say, guys? Spicy gumbo all around? Or can't you handle it?"

"WELCOME HOME," SARA said, leaning against the door-jamb of Ali's bedroom, watching her roommate unpack after over a three-week absence. "How'd it go in New York?"

"The weather was lousy. I got stomach poisoning from a fast-food stand. I had my pocketbook ripped off. The cab I took from the airport got into a fender bender with a Mercedes limo." Ali gave Sara a wry smile. "It was great. Just like I remembered."

Sara laughed. "Well, not being a native New Yorker myself, I can't exactly get what you see in putting your life on the line every time you step out on the street."

Ali picked up a white blouse from her suitcase and sniffed it. Everything smelled sooty. Tossing it into her wicker hamper, she glanced at her roommate. "There are worse hazards."

Sara nodded. "He's called a dozen times."

Ali sat down wearily on her bed. "I tried to write him at least that many times. But I couldn't. I didn't know what to say. That I sorely regretted ever having thought up The Fortune Man? That I was sorry I hadn't let him off the hook when he wanted off? That I'm quitting? I've tried that already, and it didn't end up turning out anything like I'd planned. Or maybe I did plan it. Not consciously, maybe. But okay, there was an attraction. And it just seemed to keep getting stronger. And then . . ." She flushed.

"I thought a few weeks away, a few weeks of familiar turf, all the hustle and bustle, the noise, the shoving and shouting, I'd get back on track. I thought I was sort of heading in that direction, but the minute I landed in Denver . . . I don't

know, Sara. I guess the best thing to do is call him up and tel
him it's over. All of it. Over. Because anything else jus
isn't . . . workable."

Sara waited patiently for Ali to finish her diatribe. "I think
it's too late for that, kiddo."

"What? What do you mean, 'too late'?"

Sara looked like the proverbial cat who'd just swallowed
a canary. "Don't go away." She slipped off, returning a minute later with a manila folder from which she plucked out a
clipping she'd cut out of an upscale Denver magazine. She
handed the sheet to Ali, who stared at it in stunned silence
There was Taylor, decked out in a tux, wedged between two
beautiful society women in ball gowns, both of whom were
looking up adoringly at him. And beneath the photo was the
headline: The Fortune Man Breaking Hearts At *La Bohème.*

Slowly, Ali looked up at Sara. "What's this all about?"

"There's more." Sara produced another clipping from the
folder. This one showed Taylor looking incredibly rugged
and handsome in cowboy garb à la John Wayne on top of, or
all things, a bucking bronco. There was a headline here, too
Ride 'em, Fortune Man.

Ali blinked several times. "I don't believe this. Has he gone
crazy?"

Sara grinned. "Oh, I think he's flipped, all right. Over
you."

Ali stared at the clippings in despair. "Oh, this is awful.
How could I let this happen? The big jerk. Flirting at the
opera, riding broncos. . . ."

Sara took out the last clipping. "He even entered a local
county car race."

"He doesn't even know how to drive."

Sara grinned. "He does now." She handed Ali the last
clipping. "In case you want to start your own Fortune Mar
scrapbook. Something tells me half the women in Denver are

doing just that. Last time I spoke to Taylor he told me his social calendar was so booked he hardly had time to work out the kinks in his robot."

"So, he's even cast Homer aside," Ali said morosely.

"Say, isn't this what you wanted? If you read through those clippings, you'll see that Taylor made sure that your name got mentioned each time. Which reminds me. Taylor hasn't been the only one trying to track you down. Your boss keeps calling, asking how your sick aunt in New York is doing...."

Ali smiled sheepishly. "I had to tell Chester something."

"But he's pleased as punch with how The Fortune Man campaign's been going so far. Smile, kiddo. You're back on course."

Ali felt a little dazed. "I... suppose... you're right." She stared down in wonder at the clippings.

"Oh, and Taylor told me to tell you as soon as you got back that maybe gum isn't such a bad idea, after all. I didn't get it, but he said you'd understand."

Ali was speechless, which for her was quite a how-do-you-do!

AN HOUR LATER, THERE he was, standing at her front door—or more accurately, leaning, palm flat against the doorjamb, in a suave Fred Astaire-like pose. Had he danced his way down the hall from the elevator? she wondered sardonically. Despite her nervousness, her shrewd, measuring eyes didn't miss either the obvious or the subtle changes in him. For toppers, there was his hair. It had not only been styled, but expertly streaked so that very natural-looking gold highlights shimmered amid the brown strands. Running a close second was his eyes. They were still a hazel green, but there was more depth of color, the shading was more vivid. Colored contact lenses—Ali was certain of it. And then there was the outfit: sexy, tight faded jeans, a butter-soft taffy-colored suede shirt, and cordovan penny loafers worn without socks. But even more than the hair, the eyes, or the clothes, there was a new aura radiating from Taylor himself. Confidence, virility, raw-blooded sex appeal—all of those things. This was hardly the man she remembered. Was it really only three weeks ago that she'd seen him last?

"Taylor." She addressed his open shirt collar, not quite ready to meet his eyes.

"I'm glad you're back, Ali. I've got so much to tell you."

She started to step away from the door so he could enter, but he grabbed hold of her arm. "Not here. Let's go for a drive."

"My car's garaged—"

"We'll take mine."

"Mine" turned out to be not Taylor's limo with trusty Daniel behind the wheel, but a hot little fire-engine red Ferrari. Ali gave first the sports car and then Taylor a dubious look, remembering the damage he'd done to her car when he'd been behind the wheel.

"It's such a nice day. Maybe we should walk...."

Taylor laughed. Even his laugh was different. Sexier, lightly teasing. He guided her over to the passenger side of the car and opened the door. Reluctantly, she let him help her in—not an easy feat to do gracefully.

Taylor had no trouble slipping behind the wheel. He did it with grace and flair. Like he'd been doing it for years instead of weeks.

He glanced over at her and grinned. "Relax. I got expert driving lessons from Sasha and then I even took a crash course at a sports-car racing school and graduated with honors."

"A 'crash' course?"

He laughed. A notch lower. A notch sexier. "You want to see my diploma?"

Before she could come up with either a snappy reply or a hasty retreat, he peeled out.

8

TAYLOR MIGHT HAVE LOOKED cool, calm and collected, but it was all an act. Just seeing Ali again after more than three weeks, having thought and fantasized about her constantly in her absence, made it very difficult for him to remember all of his Fortune Man lessons. He felt edgy and tongue-tied, terrified that he would slip up. And that would spell disaster. Ali had to believe he had truly changed. She had to feel fully confident about going ahead with The Fortune Man campaign. No more doubts. No more ambivalence. For either of them.

He glanced over at her as he drove along a quiet country road south of the city limits. She was looking straight ahead out the windshield, her wild tangle of auburn curls blowing every which way in the wind, her face a study in concentration. Oh, but what a face, he thought. Quirky, feisty, provocative, incredibly winning. All these past weeks, even though he hadn't been able to get her out of his mind, he'd told himself he would never let his feelings get out of hand. But now he wasn't nearly so self-assured. His palms were sweaty, his heart was pumping overtime, and he was frightened by the power of her attraction.

Ali caught his glance and manufactured a smile. "You have improved. Your driving, I mean."

He smiled back. "Thanks." He vacillated between struggling to say more or taking Sasha's advice and playing the strong, silent type. He opted for the latter.

Ali was having her own troubles. Despite all the clippings, it wasn't until now, actually seeing Taylor in the flesh, that she really bought the transformation. She found herself being both drawn to and wary of the new, slick, stylish Taylor Fortune.

"Shall we stop for a while?" he asked as they came upon a jewel of a small lake dotted with tiny islands and surrounded by mountains.

"Okay," Ali said, knowing they needed to talk.

Taylor pulled off the main road, drove down a gravel-topped side road that turned into an overgrown dirt path, and parked. There were no other cars around, no other people. Before Ali got a chance to dislodge herself from her low-slung white-leather car seat, Taylor had whipped around the car and was there to help her out. As their hands touched, they both felt the electricity. Ali withdrew her hand as soon as she was on her feet.

"I wasn't prepared for . . . all this," she admitted.

"You're not disappointed, are you?"

Ali was thrown for a loop. Even his voice was different. She could have sworn he'd never had that twang before. Okay, it was sexy. She had to admit it.

"Disappointed? No. No, just surprised. How did you. . .?"

"Practice. Practice makes perfect. Not that I don't still have a long way to go."

She was acutely aware of the way he was looking at her. Not with that awkward, boyish yearning, but a disturbingly virile lust. "Taylor. . ."

"I missed you, Ali," he said huskily. He was quite pleased with his performance, but it was hard for him to judge Ali's reaction. It seemed to him that she was still a bit wary. He took her hand. "You left so quickly the next morning."

His touch completely disarmed Ali. A tremor of desire quivered through her, but she tried mightily to ignore it, realizing how easily things could get out of hand. "I should have...told you...about my having to go to New York, but—"

"But New York wasn't on your mind that night?" He deliberately focused his eyes on her lips—a pointer from Eve.

Ali was flustered. And she didn't like being flustered. She didn't like feeling not in control. Worse still, everything had shifted in Taylor's direction. Suddenly he seemed to be holding all the cards—a winning hand.

"About that night, Taylor..."

"What about that night, Ali?" He slipped his thumbs into the pockets of his jeans, not so much to strike a sexy pose, which he did, but because his hands were a little shaky and he didn't want Ali to notice.

Ali was too busy noticing all the signs of her own discomfort. Sweaty palms, rapid heartbeat, taut muscles. "It's not that I have regrets, Taylor. I don't. But things are different now. I mean, they're not the same. We're not the same. You're not the same. And...and I'm not the same. Not that I've really changed, because I was always the same about certain things. Only I forgot about how much the same I was...about those things. But now I realize things more clearly, so I guess I am different. Which is why things can't be the same again." She finally paused for a breath. "You do see what I'm saying, don't you?"

Taylor couldn't make heads nor tails out of what she'd just said. So he thought to himself, what would The Fortune Man say? And then he realized The Fortune Man wouldn't *say* anything. As his sister-in-law, Elizabeth, had advised a couple of weeks back, "actions speak louder than words." Here was his chance to test that adage.

Without a word, he cupped her neck and brought her close to him. Ali saw what was coming, wanting it despite all her babblings to the contrary. The warm touch of his lips was firm and persuasive, not that she really needed any persuading. She was instantly flooded with desire, her lips parting, allowing the kiss to deepen. Somehow, all those vows she'd made while she was in New York, about keeping an emotional distance from Taylor, evaporated.

Taylor, who for weeks had fantasized this moment, took full advantage of it, exploring the gentle contours of her mouth with a devouring intensity, pulling her closer, feeling the natural heat of her body burning through the soft suede of his shirt.

The way he kissed her made Ali feel as if no one else in the world existed and that nothing—not even a bomb exploding right behind him—could distract him because he was so rapt in the task at hand.

It was a heady experience for Ali, but also unnerving. This kiss was strikingly different from the others they'd shared— bolder, more assertive, more . . . *experienced*.

Had he been practicing this, as well?

Just as his hands glided lower down her back to draw her closer, she jerked away, averting his face. "No, Taylor. This is no good."

He felt a surprising flash of anger. He'd worked for weeks on his new image, determined to make The Fortune Man she'd dreamed up a reality. He thought he'd done a damn good job of it. His sisters-in-law certainly seemed impressed with his progress. And he'd thrown his brothers for a loop. "Still not up to your standards?" he found himself saying.

She thought he meant the kiss, and she was even more flustered by such a direct question. "No. Yes. Oh, Taylor, I'm . . . confused."

"You're not the only one." Deflated, he looked wanly over toward the glistening blue-green lake.

For the first time today, he seemed more like his old self. "I'm not?"

"Ali, do you or do you not want me to be The Fortune Man?"

"Well...yes. Of course I do. It's a fabulous campaign ploy. It's just that I didn't think you really wanted to do it. You seemed so leery, so . . . discouraged." She raised her hand before he could speak. "Okay, okay. I was discouraged, too. I admit it. I was beginning to think you didn't have it in you. And then we both went and complicated things more by...making everything more complicated. And now that everything is so...complicated, I'm not sure what to do. And I hate not being sure of myself, Taylor."

He smiled with just the right blend of charm and sensitivity. "I know," he soothed as he took her arm and steered her along a path by the lake.

Ali relaxed a little. "You've certainly gained more confidence these past few weeks. The opera, the rodeo, sports-car racing. . . ."

"I figure The Fortune Man should be a man of the nineties. Rugged but refined, worldly but daring. A man who's sensitive but self-confident. Well, you know what I mean."

Ali gave him a crooked smile. "I'm beginning to catch on."

He slipped an arm around her shoulders. He did it in such a friendly way, she thought it would be gauche to protest.

"So, what other accomplishments have you made in my absence?" she asked.

He smiled at her. "Then you are pleased?"

She stopped and looked up at him with a big grin. "Sure, I'm pleased. You look great. You've got the ball rolling. I'll bet Homer's going to be pleased, too."

Taylor looked sheepish. "Poor Homer. He's kind of gotten lost in the shuffle."

Ali found herself actually feeling sorry for the robot. Clearly, she was on shaky ground. Pulling herself up short, she started walking again, so briskly that Taylor had to hurry to catch up to her. The thing to do, she decided, was to charge right ahead with the campaign, lose herself in it—as she always did. Work would keep her mind off *other things*. She hoped.

"Okay, I agree we're off to a great start here, Taylor." She caught his grin, and hurriedly added, "I mean, the campaign."

He wiped off the grin. "Yes. Right."

"Thanks in no small part to your hard work all these weeks."

"My grandmother and sisters-in-law helped."

"For the first time, I honestly think we can pull this off."

"Well, you laid the groundwork. And," he added, dropping his voice a notch, "you were my inspiration."

Ali knew that he meant it, which both touched her and made her uneasy. She gave him an edgy smile, then, because she was definitely in danger of losing it altogether, launched into a monologue. "Sara showed me some clippings. The press has been terrific so far, but it's still pretty local. We'll want to expand, try to get some national press. And we'll want to move into other arenas. Radio, certainly. And television. We'll have you do guest spots on some of the local talk shows, to start off. Even better, I bet I can arrange for Lilli Wells or Monte Adler to do a spot right at your store. The Fortune Man at his Fortune's. Yes, I like that. A spot like that could get picked up by syndicated TV. Really, there's no limit to how far we can take this. Hey, maybe we can even get you on Johnny— No, he's gone. Too bad. You and Johnny. It would have been a dynamite interview."

Once again, Ali was in her rapid-fire mode and Taylor was having trouble keeping up with what she was saying. "Who's Johnny?"

"Johnny Carson. But that's okay. Jay Leno isn't exactly chopped liver. Of course, there's always Arsenio. Or David

Letterman. But you'd have to be ready for that one. Any-way, that's down the road."

Taylor was relieved to hear that.

"First thing I do when we get back," she went on, "is phone Lilli Wells and schmooze with her for a while, see if we can work a deal to feature you and the store on her *Getting to Know You* show. I'd rather go with her than Adler—one, be-cause she's a woman and she'd bound to be a cream puff around you, and two, her show has better ratings than Ad-ler's *Welcome Denver*. Besides, Adler can be starchy—es-pecially when he feels he's being outshone by one of his guests."

"And you think I'd outshine him?" Taylor asked, pulling her to a stop.

"Are you fishing for a compliment here, Taylor?"

He smiled unabashedly. "Absolutely."

She nodded slowly, then stepped back, trying to keep her libido under wraps. She wasn't having an easy time of it. "Yeah, Taylor, you could outshine plenty of guys. Although I don't want you to start getting a swelled head on me."

His smile deepened, then he squinted over at the cool, glistening lake. Impulsively, he turned to Ali and said, "Let's go for a swim. It's got to be close to eighty out and I'm bak-ing in this outfit."

"You might have worn something less—"

He shook his head. "I wanted to impress you."

She grinned. "You did. It just took a while to register. The shock had to wear off a little, first."

"So, what do you say? Last one in's a rotten egg."

He was already unbuttoning his shirt.

"Taylor, I admit that it may be hot out but that water's go-ing to be positively frigid." She found her gaze inexorably drawn to his broad, tanned and very attractive chest.

"We'll warm up after we get used to it."

That was what she was afraid of.

"Taylor, I obviously don't have a bathing suit with me. And I haven't been . . . skinny-dipping . . . since my college days. And under the circumstances—I mean, given that we've . . . Which we really need to put behind us . . . Well, I don't really think . . ."

Taylor had no idea where his audacity was coming from, but he brazenly began unzipping his jeans. All he could think was that, somehow, being The Fortune Man liberated him. "You think too much, Ali. Look, if you're chicken, I'll brave the frigid water on my own. But believe me," he said, giving her a pointed look, "I really do need to cool off."

She watched him trying to wriggle out of his skintight jeans as he spoke, her composure, already shaky, collapsing altogether as his efforts turned into comical gyrations. She laughed, shaking her head. "You'll never get them off that way, Taylor. Here, lie down."

He hesitated, but only for a moment.

Ali hesitated, too. A little longer. Taylor, stretched out on the grass, was watching her, his eyes holding hers in a persuasive gaze.

"Just kick off your loafers and lie still, Taylor. And don't start getting any cute ideas." She frowned, then grabbed the cuffs of his jeans and began tugging while Taylor arched up to help. She tried to keep her eyes from moving past his knees, but by now her willpower had gone into a serious slump.

He was wearing a pair of those snug-fitting black bikinis she'd bought for him in a reckless moment. And speaking of reckless moments, she seemed to be staring another one in the face.

Taylor was feeling decidedly reckless himself. "I haven't stopped thinking about you since that night, Ali," he said softly, raising himself on his elbows.

"You shouldn't think so much." She looked away, letting go of his jeans. "There. You should be able to get them off now," she said gruffly.

Taylor sat up fully and pulled them off. Ali was standing now, her back to him. He got up and stood just behind her.

"You're not so tough," he murmured.

Ali swallowed hard. The very fact that he knew that, was what troubled her the most. She had let her guard down with Taylor. She'd let him see that vulnerable part of herself she was usually so adept at keeping under wraps. She frowned. "I'm certainly trying hard. And you should, too. It would be better for both of us."

"The Fortune Man is firm but not tough. Tough is out. Tough is eighties."

She glanced at him over her shoulder. Keeping her eyes on his face. "Tough is survival. Any decade you pick."

He grinned. "I think you're terrific, Ali."

"We still have our work cut out for us, Taylor. Maybe you won't think I'm so terrific, once we shift into high gear."

"High gear?" he echoed with a provocative smile.

Her willpower was fast moving from a slump to nonexistence. "Taylor, we have to keep this on a . . . professional basis."

"Isn't it a little late for that?"

"Okay, we slipped up. Can't we just forget . . . ?"

"I can't. Can you?"

"I'm trying." There was a little catch in her voice. "You're not making it easy."

"I'm not trying to make it easy, Ali."

"Damn it, Taylor. Since when did you get so glib?"

He pivoted her around to face him. She was grateful that at least he still had his briefs on, brief as they were.

"I *was* being glib, wasn't I?" he mused, a smile flitting across his face. "Maybe some of The Fortune Man really is rubbing off on me."

Ali thought he might be right, and she wasn't sure how she felt about that. "I think a swim might be a good idea, after all," she said. "Anyway, nobody calls me chicken and gets away with it." Suddenly, he wasn't the only one who needed to cool off. The way she was feeling, the water couldn't be cold enough to suit her.

Five minutes later, having stripped down to her bra and panties and quickly dived in, she was ready to eat her thoughts. "I'm—I'm—freezing," she stammered, as her head surfaced from beneath the water.

Taylor, who had dived in a moment before her, was also freezing. "Let's—swim a few—laps. We'll—warm up."

They were both strong swimmers and after a few minutes their bodies did begin to acclimatize to the cold.

He swam up to her, treading water. "Our first swim together. Feels great, doesn't it?" He wore a goofy smile that reminded her of the Taylor Fortune she'd first met.

"Oh, Taylor, I don't know what I'm going to do about you," she said with a soft sigh.

He moved a little closer, his arm slipping around her bare waist. "Are you open to suggestions?"

Before she could reply, he lightly ran his tongue over her still-quivering lips—only now they weren't quivering from the cold water but from the heat Taylor was generating. She didn't know how much longer either of them could continue treading water, literally or figuratively. Confounded by the swarm of emotions tearing through her, she felt her flagging willpower drop another notch as her fingers seemed to find their way into his wet hair of their own accord.

Taylor, once so constrained, now felt outrageously daring and incredibly aroused as he pressed her closer to him, kiss-

ing her feverishly, his fingers finding their way to the catch
of her bra. Ali was too far gone to protest, even while her bra
went floating away.

Taylor lifted her up until her breasts were exposed, capturing one nipple, then the other in his hungry mouth, his
tongue driving her wild as it alternately tugged and flicked
over the tender buds.

The next thing she knew, both his black bikini briefs and
her silk panties were drifting off toward a small island in the
center of the lake and his hard, naked body was pressed
against her own. Ali felt drugged as she clung to him, deli-
ciously weightless.

And then she spotted a group of teenagers walking along
the grass at the lake's edge. She gasped, abruptly pulling
away.

"What's wrong?" Taylor asked.

"Look."

When he saw the teens, he scowled. "What are they doing
here?"

Ali gave him a wry look. "The question is, what are we
doing here? And how do we get out of here before we're
spotted?"

Taylor was well aware of their predicament. They certainly couldn't swim back to shore and step out of the lake
stark naked with those kids there.

"Maybe they won't stay long," Taylor said hopefully.

"Isn't that a picnic basket one of them is carrying?"

Taylor frowned as he saw that was precisely what it was.

"We can't stay in the water much longer. We'll get . . .
hypothermia."

Taylor agreed. "I think our best bet is to swim for the island. They probably won't stay more than a couple of hours,
and it will still be early enough in the day for us to swim back
to shore without freezing our—"

"Bare butts off?" Ali quipped ruefully.

"I GUESS WE CAN TRY TO pretend we're members of a nudist colony," Ali deadpanned. "Anyone for volleyball?"

Taylor felt both physically and emotionally exposed. "Where's a fig leaf when you need one?"

Ali laughed dryly. "And I had to prove I wasn't a chicken."

"I'm sorry, Ali," Taylor said, smiling sheepishly. "I got carried away. I can't believe I was actually...putting the make on you." He was surprised to see her smile.

"You weren't doing a half-bad job of it."

Taylor looked rather proud of himself. "I wasn't, was I?"

They both made a concerted effort not to stare at each other.

"This is pretty awkward," Taylor muttered.

Despite the sun, they were both shivering.

"We do get into the oddest predicaments," she said with a smile.

"Are you cold?" he asked.

She had her arms folded across her chest. "A little." There was a pause. "Are you?"

"A little."

Taylor glanced back toward shore from behind a tree. "They're still there."

"Let's just hope they don't decide to swim out here."

"That would be . . . awkward."

There was a long silence.

"So, how was . . . New York?" Taylor asked finally, trying to sound nonchalant.

"Oh . . . hectic," she answered with forced lightness.

"Did you visit family or . . . friends?"

"My dad lives down in Florida now. And my mother's traveling abroad with her new boyfriend. Last I heard, they were in Venice."

"And your sisters?"

"Cara's down in the Bahamas, recuperating from her last divorce. I did see my sister, Julie."

"The one working on her second marriage?"

Ali was surprised he remembered. "Yes."

"So how's it going?"

"They have their ups and downs."

There was another long, awkward silence.

"And . . . friends?" Taylor asked.

"Oh, I guess they have friends."

"No. I meant you."

"Do I have friends?"

"Did you see any old friends in New York?"

"Oh. You know. A few."

"Anyone . . . special?"

She smiled. "No. No one special, Taylor."

They fell silent again. It was Ali who finally broke it with a laugh. "This is so crazy. I mean, here we are trying to make polite chitchat and somehow pretend not to notice that we're naked as blue jays."

"I keep asking myself what The Fortune Man would do in a situation like this."

They both had a pretty good idea what he'd do.

"Ali." Taylor made a tentative step toward her but she backed up, covering her body with her arms as best she could.

"It isn't that I'm not tempted, Taylor. I am. But it would really be a dumb move. We'd both risk paying too big a price if things got out of hand." She tried to sound as cool and in control as possible, which, given that she was stark naked and giving this lecture to a man who was also stark naked, wasn't easy, to say the least. But Ali was determined to give it her best shot. "I've worked damn hard to get where I am, Taylor, and I did it on my own. I never let anyone distract me.

And now I have a chance to make it to the top." A smile curved her lips. "Only it turns out that my big chance is my biggest distraction."

He smiled. "I don't think I've ever been anyone's distraction before. It feels kind of nice."

"Taylor, haven't you been listening to a word I've said?" Her tone wasn't so much sharp as dismayed. She needed a little support here. She needed him to be on her side. On her rational, practical, play-it-safe-rather-than-sorry side.

He smiled winsomely. "I was too distracted to concentrate."

"Please don't seduce me, Taylor. I'm only...human."

"We're *both* only human, Ali."

"Why is this happening to me? This never happens to me, Taylor."

"This never happens to me, either," he murmured, stepping closer.

This time she didn't back away.

They were inches apart. "You're so beautiful, Ali."

Her hand touched his cheek. "Oh, Taylor, you have a fortune and no sense at all."

"I want to make love with you again, Ali. Right now, that makes all the sense in the world to me. Even if it doesn't make any sense at all." The drawl was gone, the glibness was gone. She saw in his eyes only a touching candor and a golden tenderness.

He enfolded her in his arms—clumsily, almost shyly.

And that was when she knew she'd lost the battle. "I guess maybe I shouldn't even try to make sense of this," she said as she framed his face in her hands and brought her lips to his.

He may have gotten off to a timid start, but as soon as their lips touched, Taylor felt emboldened. He drew her closer, deepening the kiss, moving his hands to her breasts.

Gently, he took her hand and guided her to an even more secluded spot on the tiny island, and eased her down in the tall, verdant grass that was warm from the sun overhead. He smiled as he lay down beside her.

"What are you smiling about?" she asked.

"I feel a little like Adam and Eve. The original ones. In the Garden of Eden."

Ali smiled back. It did seem new and wondrous, this feeling. This feeling she'd spent three weeks trying not to think about. This feeling that she'd probably spend the next three weeks trying to suppress, as well. But now, right now, this feeling was all-consuming; it radiated inside her, setting off sparks, igniting her.

They lay facing each other, smiling, touching, caressing. It was strange to feel so open to a man, but not exposed. "You're so tanned. No, golden," she murmured as she stroked his chest.

"Three weeks of sunlamp treatment."

"I feel so . . . white."

"No. Cream. You're the color of cream. Whipped cream. I love whipped cream." He dipped his head and lightly licked a line down between her breasts. "You taste better than whipped cream."

He licked a path back up, over her throat and chin. Then he moved on to her lips, the tip of her nose, her eyelids, her eyelashes.

"How did you get that scar?" he asked.

"A guy I knew."

Taylor's head jerked up. "A guy hit you?" He felt a flash of blind fury.

Seeing his reaction, she immediately felt guilty. "When I was seven. He was eight. We were having a snowball fight. And he accidentally made one that had a piece of rock in it. He felt worse about it than I did, honestly."

"Because you're tough, right?" Taylor teased softly, kissing the scar tenderly.

"I feel about as tough as jelly right now," she confessed. Because what was the point of denying it—he seemed to be able to see right through her.

He touched her breasts, gently circling each nipple. Then he moved over her, rising on his hands to look down on her, his warm breath fanning her face.

"I love your freckles."

She scrunched her nose. "I've always hated them."

He kissed a line from her cheek over the bridge of her nose to her other cheek. "You won't anymore."

She sighed. He was probably right.

"Oh, Taylor . . ."

He smiled and then he lowered himself down until they were pressed together, until they were all longing, all heart. Ali was stunned by the intensity of her feelings. What was it about this man?

With Taylor, there were no studied sexual techniques, no show of masculine prowess. In his excitement, he moved against her arrhythmically, so that a couple of times their bodies collided. And yet nothing compared to making love with him. Never had Ali felt so free, so uninhibited, so utterly passionate.

She held him tight, then raised her arms high over her head, arching into him, opening to receive him, as their bodies found their own natural rhythm. They looked at each other, their faces glowing with ecstasy. And then, at last, overcome by wave after wave of inordinate pleasure, they closed their eyes in rapture and cried out in inarticulate delight.

Within minutes they both fell asleep, nestled in each other's arms. They were awakened close to an hour later by the sound of sirens. Was there a brush fire? An accident?

Taylor went to have a look. A minute later he came back, looking quite upset.

"What is it?" Ali asked anxiously.

"You're not going to believe this."

Ali took a steadying breath. "Let me have it."

"The police are here."

"Police?"

"And . . . my brothers."

"Your . . . brothers?" Ali stared at him in complete bafflement. "What are they. . . ?" And then, before she finished, the answer in all its nauseating clarity dawned on her. "Oh, God. Those teenagers must have found our clothes, seen the car, figured there was a swimming accident, and called the police."

"And the police must have identified me through the license plate and notified my brothers."

"Oh, Taylor . . ."

"They're out on the lake . . . looking for us. They probably think we're . . . dead."

Just then, they heard someone shout from the lake, "Hey, I found something." There was a pause. "It's a bra."

Ali stared mournfully at Taylor's naked body and then down at her own. "Right now I wish I were dead."

9

NEITHER OF THEM SAID a word for the first fifteen minutes of the return drive to Denver. Taylor drove with sober care, Ali sitting beside him, her head turned away. He knew she was terribly upset even though he had done his best to preserve at least a shred of her dignity by swimming out to the motorboat before the two cops and all three of his brothers docked and discovered them in all their naked splendor on the island.

Ali, huddled in a corner of the car, staring into space, knew Taylor had done his best. Still, she could imagine what he must have told his brothers and the police while she'd remained hidden from sight in a crouched position behind a tree. Not that she'd questioned him when he returned alone a few minutes later with two blankets, explaining that their carelessly discarded clothing had been taken by a couple of the teenagers to the police station. Even though she'd stepped into the waiting boat covered from head to toe by the itchy woolen blanket, Ali had never felt so exposed, so naked, so humiliated in all her life. None of Taylor's brothers made eye contact with her, but the two cops were both grinning from ear to ear.

And even that wasn't the worst part. When they got back to shore, they were bombarded by a slew of reporters and photographers. The Fortune brothers and the cops did their best to keep the paparazzi at bay, but several shots were snapped of the fleeing pair wrapped in their blankets as they hightailed it to the Ferrari. This time, when Taylor roared off, Ali felt only relief.

As they drove, the relief faded, giving way to an edgy tension. The constrained silence was getting to Taylor. "Ali, I'm sorry."

She made a faint noncommunicative gesture with her head.

"As soon as we get back I'll phone my lawyer and see if he can do something to keep the newspapers from—"

"Freedom of the press."

"Do you think this will . . . hurt . . . The Fortune Man campaign?"

"It wasn't exactly a slick departure."

"Well, we'll just have to—"

Ali shook her head. "Please, Taylor. Not now." It wasn't the photos that would be emblazoned across the front pages of tomorrow's tabloids that were worrying her now. It was her own jumble of feelings.

Taylor shifted back into silence. And then, after a few minutes, he started to smile. Ali caught the smile.

"I don't find any of this amusing," she snapped. "And I find it particularly irritating that you do."

Taylor was immediately contrite. "Oh, I wasn't smiling about . . . that. It's just that . . . Well, something similar actually happened to my brother Peter and Elizabeth. Pete told me about this time when they were boating on a lake and . . . somehow their clothes got . . . tossed overboard and . . . the motor on their boat died."

"And you and your brothers and half the Denver police force rescued them?"

"Well . . . no. But the owner of the inn where they were staying . . . I guess it wasn't exactly the same thing."

"No," Ali muttered. "I guess not."

They both fell silent again until they passed the city limits, at which point Ali gave Taylor a nervous sideways glance. "I

can't walk into my apartment building wearing this . . .
serape."

Taylor nodded. "We can go back to my place and you can
borrow a pair of my jeans and a shirt. Or I could get you
something from my grandmother. . . ."

"Jeans and a shirt will be fine." Ali had no desire to experience humiliation in front of yet another member of the Fortune clan.

Ten minutes later Taylor pulled up in front of his carriage
house and the two made a beeline for the front door. Even
after they got inside, they were both edgy.

"I'll just go and get you . . . the jeans. And a shirt."

As Taylor started off, his blanket tucked around his body
toga-fashion, Ali snuck her hand out of her blanket and
placed it on his bare shoulder. But just for a moment. Then
she quickly clutched the top of her own blanket.

"Taylor."

"Yes?"

She stared at him, breathing unevenly, fighting back tears.
Taylor stared back. He wasn't breathing at all.

The air felt charged.

"Nothing's gone right," she said hoarsely. "I've made a
mess of it."

"No."

"Yes," she insisted.

"Then I'm just as much to blame," Taylor countered.

Ali shook her head. A few tears slipped out and she swiped
at them.

"Ali . . ."

"This isn't going to work, Taylor."

"Because of a few photos . . . ?"

"No. Because . . . because . . ." The truth was, it was because she was falling in love with him. But there was no way
she could admit that—even to herself.

"Because we get too distracted?" Taylor was smiling.

"Yes. And it isn't funny," she retorted.

"I don't think it's funny." What did he think? That she drove him wild? That she was the most vital, the most important thing that had ever happened to him? That he cared deeply about her? That they had begun something here that he didn't want to end? He didn't realize that he was still smiling.

Ali didn't understand the smile. It threatened her. It angered her. She glared at him. A minute ago she'd been willing to shoulder the blame—all of it—but now she felt quite irrationally that it was all his fault. He'd seduced her—not with his new, stylish clothes or his new hair color, or the glib lines he'd been learning these past three weeks. No, he'd done it with his goofy smile, his endearing innocence, his desire to please, his tenderness, his passion. . . .

"Oh, Taylor, you're hopeless," she cried out and stormed past him.

He made a grab for her but came up with a fistful of blanket. Ali's own grip on the blanket wasn't nearly as secure and the next thing she knew, she was standing a foot away from him—stark naked.

"Ali . . ." He saw that she was close to tears again and he tried to thrust the blanket back over her. But she was so distraught she ignored his efforts, stepping back, her eyes narrowing into slits, her hands on her hips.

"This is what I mean. This is exactly what I mean. Now do you see? Now do you understand?" As she hissed out the words, she kept backing up. "I must have been crazy. I must have been out of my mind to think that I could pull this off. I don't know what it is about you. . . ." *Liar, liar.* "I don't want to know. Ever since I first set eyes on you, it's been nothing but disaster, humiliation, embarrassment. . . ." *Liar, liar.* "I've been working too hard. I've been putting myself under too much pressure. My body just…rebelled." *And my heart….*

"Ali."

She raised her hand. "No, Taylor. Don't say anything. It's best not to talk."

He couldn't help smiling—any more than he could help becoming aroused all over again as she stood there, exquisitely naked, desperately fighting for control.

She lost the fight. Tears began to slide down her cheeks.

Taylor's arousal didn't subside, but now he felt a rush of tenderness. "Don't cry, Ali." He wanted to reach out for her, enfold her in his arms, but he knew that would be a dangerous move. For both of them.

"All I want is to get some clothes on and get out of here." She backed into a doorknob, then quickly grabbed for it, thrusting the door open, thinking it was Taylor's bedroom—only, it was the kitchen.

She slowly turned around and gave Taylor a lost look. "I can't remember where your bedroom is," she said weakly.

He pointed across the room—and handed her back the blanket. She threw it around herself and dashed past him.

"Help yourself to anything—" she slammed his bedroom door closed before he finished the sentence "—you want."

While Ali was in his bedroom, Taylor went down to his basement lab and threw on a pair of work pants and an old grease-stained sweatshirt that he had tucked away in a closet. He came back upstairs ten minutes later. His bedroom door was still closed.

It was very quiet. Taylor was afraid Ali had taken off again without a word. He knocked softly on his door.

At first there was no answer.

He knocked again.

The door slowly opened. Ali stood there in an oversize white shirt and a pair of his jeans that she'd had to roll up several times and cinch at her waist by knotting one of his belts.

"I feel ridiculous," she muttered.

"You look fine." *Better than fine*, he thought, but for her sake as well as his own, he didn't risk saying it.

"Oh, not the clothes. My...behavior."

Taylor didn't say anything. He wasn't sure what she was referring to. Her behavior on the island? Her behavior since they'd left the island?

"I'm sorry I got so . . . carried away," she said, stepping out of the bedroom, her face composed, her chin jutting out slightly in that ready-to-defy-the-world gesture.

Taylor still said nothing. He still wasn't sure what she was talking about. But now she was looking at him, wanting some kind of response.

He cleared his throat. "Well, I guess we both...got carried away," he said finally, maintaining the same ambiguity.

"The thing is...even separate from my feelings about not wanting to get involved in a serious relationship and your...situation..."

Taylor lifted a brow. "The tontine?"

She nodded, the tip of her tongue darting out to wet her dry lips. "My point is...we have nothing in common, Taylor—" she gave him a sardonic look "—except that we're wrong for each other."

Taylor smiled.

This time Ali didn't attack his smile. She understood it. Wrong for each other though they might be, it wasn't all they had in common. There was the not-so-small matter of *s-e-x!* There was no denying that the pleasure they took in that was shared equally.

Ali decided to skirt the topic. Instead, she busied herself by rolling up the cuffs of her shirtsleeves and muttered, "Look, Taylor, I still think The Fortune Man campaign is a solid idea. Any publicist worth his salt could turn the photos that show up in tomorrow's papers in your favor. After all, it doesn't hurt your image for The Fortune Man to be seen as a lady-killer. Why, his appeal is so . . . potent, he's even managed to . . . compromise his . . . ex-publicist—"

"Ex?"

"I'm saying that if you still want to go ahead with the campaign—which I think you should—you ought to go with another publicist. I'm sure Doug Chester himself—that's my boss—would be glad to jump in and orchestrate the campaign. Or there are several other people in the office—"

"You mean you're quitting."

"I'm making a recommendation."

"What if I don't like your recommendation?"

"You're free to hire anyone you want. I'm sure Steve Dennis would give his right arm—"

"Isn't that the guy you were with at the gallery? That sleaze who put the make on you?"

"He's not a sleaze. He's a very good publicist. I'm sure he'd do a terrific job."

"You must really be running scared," Taylor said, leveling his gaze on her.

"I'm being practical, sensible—"

"Chicken."

Ali laughed dryly. "You don't really think I'll fall for that one again, do you?"

"Cluck, cluck, cluck . . ."

"You're being positively childish."

"Cluck, cluck . . ."

She threw her head back defiantly. "I am not chicken, Taylor Fortune. I should think you'd want to go with another publicist as much, if not more, than I want you to. I'm not the only one who let herself get in over her head. You did, too. And if what's happened doesn't alarm you, I'm sure it's alarming the hell out of your brothers. And the only way you're going to relieve their anxieties is to drop me. I'm just making it easy for you."

"You're even willing to hand me off to a competitor."

Ali swallowed hard. "Well, naturally, I'd prefer that you went with someone from my firm—"

"And what are you going to tell your boss, Mr. Chester, about why you're not handling me anymore?"

She felt her face heat up. "One glance at tomorrow's front page and I doubt he'll ask me for an explanation." She looked away. He might, however, ask for her resignation. Especially if Taylor actually went and took the deal to another firm. She closed her eyes. What a complete mess she'd made of everything.

"I want *you*, Ali."

Her eyes shot open. "What?"

"I want you to be my publicist."

She looked at him questioningly. "Because you think Chester might can me? You're trying to save my neck, aren't you, Taylor?"

She knew any other guy would have come back with something glib, like, "It's a very attractive neck, sweetheart." But not Taylor. He gave her a very earnest look and said, "I'm trying to be a smart businessman, Ali. You're an ace publicist who came up with a great scheme to market Homer and increase my sales across the board—maybe, if I'm lucky, even have them skyrocket. I want that to happen. And I don't think I can make it happen without you. I need you in order for me to dare to be The Fortune Man. It seems to me we both win out in the end."

"As long as we don't . . ." She averted her eyes.

He gave her a slight smile. "We won't."

She forced herself to look directly at him. "I mean it, Taylor. Not ever again. This would have to be strictly business from here on out. I'm just not good at juggling a personal and professional relationship. It keeps backfiring. And even if I were to want to eventually get involved with someone, I wouldn't want to—"

"Get involved with a man who's all wrong for you."

"Yes. I mean—"

"I understand, Ali. Anyway, I've got responsibilities and obligations—the business, Homer, several other projects on the drawing board. And let's not forget the tontine. I couldn't offer you any future even if it was something we both wanted."

"Which we don't," Ali said quickly, disturbed to hear that her remark had the ring of a question in it.

"I guess we both got off track for a while and it's time to—"

"Get back on course?" she finished off eagerly.

He smiled with relief. "Exactly."

She hesitated. "Gossip's going to run rampant about us after the papers come out tomorrow."

He grinned. "Like you said, it'll just enhance my Fortune Man image as a lady-killer." The grin faded and he gave her a sympathetic look. "Of course, it will be . . . awkward for you."

She gave her head a little shake, her curls bobbing every which way. "I can handle it. My colleagues will probably all think I orchestrated the whole episode for publicity."

He loved seeing the sparkle back in her eyes. "They'll think you're brilliant."

She grinned. "I *am* brilliant."

Taylor didn't argue.

TAYLOR WAS REDOING one of Homer's circuit boards that evening when there was a knock on his door. When he opened it he was disconcerted but not surprised to see his three brothers standing there.

"Is it Christmas already?" Taylor quipped.

Adam, Peter and Tru gave him puzzled looks.

"I take it you're the Three Wise Men. . . ."

"Cute, Taylor. Very cute," Adam muttered as they came inside.

"Not as cute as that little stunt you pulled today down at the lake," Tru said dryly.

Peter gave him a long, solemn look. "You of all people, Taylor."

Taylor folded his arms across his chest. "Really, boys, talk about the pot calling the kettle black."

"We're talking about calling the kettle *empty*," Adam retorted.

"Look," Taylor said indignantly, "what happened between me and Ali on that island is our business—"

"Oh, I think we're quite capable of putting two and two together, Taylor," Tru said, stretching out on a sofa.

"You're right. It *is* your business, Taylor," Peter said. "And if you are in love with Ali Spencer, then—"

"Are you in love with her?" Adam broke in.

There was dead silence.

It was Tru, and not Taylor, who broke it. "You haven't gone and . . . proposed to her?"

Taylor stared at Tru but said nothing.

Tru glanced nervously at Peter and Adam.

Peter sat down on a striped armchair, and leaning forward, both feet placed squarely on the floor, looked up at Taylor who stood with his arms still crossed over his chest.

Peter smiled. "Love sure seems to hit us Fortune boys hard, all right. Why should you be different? And where do we come off expecting you to be?"

Taylor slowly let his arms drop, his hands slipping into his pockets. Out of the corner of his eye he caught Tru and Adam scowling, but he smiled back at Peter. "I know where you come off," he murmured. "But thanks."

Adam exhaled a breath and smiled sheepishly. "I guess we are being damn selfish. When we got struck by Cupid's bow, we certainly let Fortune's slip through our hands without a fight."

"And without any regrets," Tru admitted, walking over to Taylor and placing a hand lightly on his shoulder.

"I guess," Peter said, "part of the problem is that you've always been so...innocent when it came to women. We aren't just thinking about Fortune's now, Taylor. We're thinking about you. We don't want to see you get hurt. We don't want to see you get in over your head. And Ali Spencer is . . ."

Taylor gave him a rueful smile. "All wrong for me?"

The three brothers shared nervous looks that were all the answer Taylor needed.

"Well, don't worry. She said the very same thing." Taylor's tone was light, but from the way all three of his brothers were looking at him, he knew that they knew he wasn't taking it lightly.

Taylor sighed. "Look, I have no intention of proposing to Ali. And even if I did, believe me, she wouldn't say yes. So you can stop worrying. Ali and I both agree that we should stick strictly to our business game plan. As a matter of fact, Ali called just a few minutes ago to tell me Lilli Wells, of that local morning interview show *Getting to Know You*, is going to feature me at Fortune's a week from Monday."

All three brothers stared at him in surprise. "You're going to be on television?" Tru seemed to need further confirmation.

Peter scowled. "Are you ready for something like that?"

"Yeah," Adam said. "Are you sure it's a smart move?"

Taylor shrugged. Lately he hadn't been sure of anything. But that hadn't been much of a deterrent thus far.

"IS THIS REALLY necessary?" Taylor asked the pretty young blonde who was dabbing his face with powder as he sat in a director's chair amid a slew of lights in the men's department of Fortune's.

She winked at him. "You don't want two million people seeing you with a shiny face, Mr. Fortune."

Taylor gave her a sickly look. "Two million?"

Just then, the director of *Getting to Know You*, a nervous little man with thinning hair, passed by. He stopped and scowled at Taylor. "More rouge," he snapped.

The blonde smiled at Taylor. "Just a little dab. Really, you're going to look great on TV," she soothed as she grabbed hold of his chin and began applying a peach tint to his cheeks.

Taylor began to have second thoughts. Maybe this whole TV appearance was a bad idea. There was no script. He hadn't even been given a list of questions he might be asked. The producer had explained that Lilli Wells liked to work off the cuff. Just as Taylor was telling him that he'd feel a lot more comfortable knowing what they'd be discussing, the talk-show hostess herself—an attractive porcelain-skinned brunette in her late thirties—stopped by to introduce herself, flash him a smile, and tell him not to worry. She was a pro. Before he could protest that *he* wasn't, she raced off for a powwow with her director.

"Oh, no," the blonde muttered. "You don't want to sweat, Mr. Fortune. It's going to make streaks in the Pan-Cake base."

He raised his eyes to her concerned face. "Pancake?"

She grinned as she began dabbing on more powder across his brow. "Not the kind you eat. That's what we call the makeup I put on as an undercoat."

"Please," he said, wrenching her hand from his jaw, "that's enough. I need to find—" And then he saw Ali standing over by the Persian-rugs department talking with a photographer. "Excuse me," he said, taking off before the cosmetician had the chance to remove the large white bib she'd draped over his pale gray Christian Dior suit.

"Ali."

She turned from the photographer. "You've only got about five minutes to airtime. How are you feeling?"

"How am I feeling? I'm a wreck. Look at me. They've got me made up to look like a clown."

She grinned. "You'll look like a Greek Adonis on TV." She gently tugged off the bib then addressed the photographer. "Dan, how about getting a picture of Taylor with one of these hanging Persian rugs as a backdrop?"

Taylor took hold of her arm. "Please, Ali. Not now. Can we . . . talk privately?"

"You don't have much time," she said as the photographer, taking his cue from her, sauntered off.

"I don't know about this whole thing, Ali. I'm not good at ad-libbing. What if I say something stupid? What if I make a complete fool of myself?"

"You won't, Taylor. You're just experiencing stage fright. It's perfectly natural."

"There's nothing natural about this," he muttered.

"Come on, Taylor. You're The Fortune Man, remember? All you've got to do is smile and be charming. You already look the part. They're going to love you."

"You think so?"

"Yes." Her voice quavered. She felt light-headed, a little dizzy. *Just some of Taylor's anxiety rubbing off*, she lied to herself.

"Two minutes. Places everybody," a squeaky-voiced assistant director shouted.

"Break a leg, Taylor."

He gave her a bemused look.

"It's for luck."

He nodded slowly. Then, just as he was about to turn, she impetuously kissed him on the lips. Just for luck.

"SO WHAT IS IT LIKE to be Denver's most eligible bachelor?" Lilli Wells asked Taylor as they strolled through the furniture department, five minutes into the show.

He stopped and drawled, "I believe it would be more accurate to call me Denver's most *ineligible* bachelor, Miss Wells." There was a brief pause, then another compelling smile, this one half boyish, half roguish. "Unfortunately."

Lilli trilled a laugh right on cue at the pun, then smiled seductively, turning from Taylor to camera three. "'Unfortunately' is right. Isn't that so, ladies?" she cooed, slipping a hand through his arm. . . .

THE FORTUNE CLAN, gathered around Jessica's TV in the den, watched in amazement as Taylor proceeded to charm the pants off Lilli Wells and the entire female viewing population of Denver.

"I don't believe this," Adam muttered.

"He looks so cool and in charge," Elizabeth murmured.

"And that self-effacing charm," Eve added with delight, "makes him seem so . . . approachable."

"Yes, he doesn't come across at all smug," Jessica said, smiling with pride.

Ben took her hand. "He's doing exceedingly well. I must confess I never pictured Taylor as a television personality. But he seems quite at home in front of a camera."

"The Fortune Man," Sasha mused. "Yes, it suits him."

"I never would have thought he could pull something like this off," Tru admitted.

"This could be quite a boon for business," Peter conceded.

"Yes," Eve said, eyeing all of Taylor's brothers in turn. "Thanks to Ali Spencer."

ALI, STANDING JUST behind one of the associate producers, groaned as Taylor guided the talk-show hostess over to the Fortune's kitchen department where Homer was standing at a stove. She had tried to talk Taylor out of having the robot make an appearance, but he'd insisted that this would be a great chance to introduce Homer to the public. The question was, was the public ready for Homer?

"Oh, he's absolutely adorable!" Lilli Wells exclaimed. "Homer. What a perfect name for a robot who does all those dreary household chores we all hate doing. You didn't really invent him all by yourself?"

Taylor gave her a jaunty smile. "Believe me, he gave me a hard time. But he's quite domesticated now. Would you like a demonstration?"

This time Ali's groan was loud enough to warrant a severe look from the director. Why, she thought, just when everything was going so well, did he have to bring out that mechanical monster? She could just see Homer scooping an astonished and not-very-amused Lilli Wells up in its big, strong grip. Now, if Taylor were to pull that sort of stunt, Ali had no doubt that Lilli would be tickled pink. The talk-show hostess was clearly taken with The Fortune Man. And why not? Taylor was playing the part as if he'd been born to it. Ali knew she should be thrilled, but for some perverse reason it irritated her that he was doing so well.

"I have to confess Homer here's caused me a few embarrassing moments," Taylor was explaining as he approached the robot.

Oh, no, Ali thought. *He isn't going to tell—*

"You must tell me," Lilli, who was right on his heels, cooed.

He smiled wryly. "You and a million viewers?"

"Well, maybe some things are best told in private," she answered coyly.

"WILL YOU LOOK AT THAT," Peter marveled as he stared at the TV. "Homer actually whipped up a cake without a hitch."

"And look at the polishing job he did on the maple table," Eve pointed out.

Adam rubbed his jaw. "You know, that robot could be a gold mine."

Jessica gave her grandsons haughty glances. "As I always said, they all laughed at Christopher Columbus, too. And he got the last laugh, just like Taylor will."

Tru smile sheepishly. "You've got to admit, Grandma, there have been some Fortune follies along the way."

"Oh, look," Elizabeth broke in. "Homer's left foot is actually a vacuum cleaner. How clever."

"HOW CLEVER," Lilli Wells exclaimed as Homer's left foot proceeded to vacuum up a small pile of sawdust.

"Of course, Homer's just the prototype," Taylor explained. "But, if there's enough demand, I could have Homers in every Fortune's store by Christmas."

Lilli Wells gave Taylor a fawning smile. "I'm sure all my viewers out there will agree with me, Taylor Fortune, when I say that you're not only Denver's most charming bachelor, but its most brilliant."

Taylor's smile sizzled. "You're too kind, Lilli," he murmured in a sexy, devastating drawl. "And to think I was actually nervous before I came on your show today."

"Well, you certainly fooled me," Lilli said, leading Taylor over to a small nearby sofa where they could conclude the interview.

"And me," Ali muttered under her breath.

"This is one segment I'm sure our viewers hate to see drawing to a close, Taylor. But there's one last thing I must ask you or I know our *Getting to Know You* viewers will never forgive me," Lilli said, looking at him pointedly. "All three of your brothers in turn gave up their fortunes for love, Taylor. So, confide in us, is there any woman at all out there who might tempt you to do the same?"

For the first time in the interview, Taylor faltered. He was thrown off guard by the question. He hadn't expected it. Stupid of him. Reflexively, his gaze shifted past the cameras and over to Ali. She stared back.

Lilli followed his gaze and then flashed a wry smile at Taylor. "I'm not talking publicity stunts here, Taylor."

It took all his effort to take his eyes off Ali even after she'd looked away. He finally turned back to the talk-show hostess with a smile of forced nonchalance. "I'm afraid, as the last Fortune heir, I simply can't afford to be tempted."

He hoped that would suffice, but Lilli Wells wasn't about to let him off the hook that easily. A small matter of ratings. "Well, give our single gals out there a glimmer of hope, Taylor. I'm sure they're already fantasizing being the woman for whom The Fortune Man would give up his kingdom. So, what kind of woman would she have to be?"

"OH, DEAR, HE DOES LOOK uncomfortable," Jessica remarked.

"What do you think of the way Lilli Wells dismissed his involvement with Ali as nothing more than a publicity stunt?" Eve questioned.

"If only we could," Tru muttered.

Adam and Pete nodded.

The women all scowled at the men, then turned anxiously back to the television screen to see what answer Taylor would give.

ALI WAS WATCHING Taylor live, with the same tense anxiety and anticipation. She felt for him. Lilli Wells had really put him on the spot. She knew Taylor hadn't expected it. The interview was almost over and he had to have been thinking it was going to be smooth sailing right to the finish line. But smooth sailing didn't make for top ratings.

Lilli persisted. "Come on, Taylor. You can't disappoint our loyal viewers. What kind of woman would steal the heart of The Fortune Man?"

Taylor knew the talk-show hostess would pursue him until he came up with something. Besides, he'd done so well up to this point, to clam up now would mean losing all that ground he'd gained.

Okay, he told himself. *Think Fortune Man. This is just a performance. Show Ali that you can make it an Oscar-winning one.*

Intensely conscious of Ali's eyes on him even though he focused his gaze on Lilli, Taylor tilted his head to one side and produced a sexy, outlaw smile. "What kind of woman would she have to be?" he echoed, lowering his voice a notch. "Why, I guess I can tell you in one word."

Lilli Wells leaned forward eagerly. "One word?"

"One word. And that word is . . ." He paused, not only for effect but for time. "Irresistible."

And then, just as Taylor had hoped, before Lilli could probe any further, the director's voice shouted, "Cut. And that's a wrap."

When Taylor looked out past the cameras again, Ali was gone.

10

THE LOW BUZZ OF PARTY conversation picked up new mo-
mentum as Taylor and Lilli Wells entered the room. Lilli,
looking very striking in a red satin off-the-shoulder taffeta
cocktail dress, certainly attracted a fair share of interest, but
there was no doubt that Taylor was the center of attention.
Every woman in the room let her gaze drift appreciatively
over The Fortune Man, who was dressed to the nines in a
white custom-tailored dinner jacket and black tuxedo trousers.

Jill Barnett made her way through the clusters of guests and
bussed Taylor on the cheek, while Lilli looked on with pro-
prietary concern. "Great-looking jacket. Armani?"

Taylor grinned. "No. Feldstein."

"Feldstein? He must be new."

"He's about seventy-three. And my grandmother swears
by him. Says he's the best tailor west of the Mississippi."

Jill smiled coyly. "No way. You're the best 'Taylor' in the
West, in my book."

Taylor flashed her his best Fortune Man grin. "You'll have
to let me read that book sometime."

A GROUP OF WOMEN standing together in one corner of the
room took in the handsome, polished new arrival with avid
fascination.

"*That's* Taylor Fortune?" one of them exclaimed. "Why, I
met him at his brother Tru's wedding last year, and he looked
completely different. Rather bland and terribly awkward.

Nothing like his three gorgeous brothers. I remember he kept patting his pockets all evening, muttering and then scribbling things on little bits of paper. Your typical dopey genius."

"He certainly doesn't look dopey now."

"I should say not. It's quite a transformation."

"I caught him on Lilli Wells's show a couple of weeks ago and he was positively arresting. If the man weren't a business tycoon, he could be a movie star."

"Lilli certainly didn't waste any time making her move. Do you think he really finds her—"

"Irresistible?"

"I doubt it. I hear he's out with a different woman every night."

"Who wouldn't want to be the one woman in the world that The Fortune Man simply couldn't resist?"

They all looked at each other and smiled dreamily.

THE WOMEN WEREN'T THE only ones at the party buzzing about Taylor. A lot of the male guests had their own observations to make.

"I hear sales have skyrocketed at Fortune's since this whole Fortune Man campaign got off the ground."

"Yeah, the money's rolling in. I predict that robot of his will be the hit of the Christmas season. My wife's already put in her order. And she says all her friends have Homer on their lists, too."

"He's certainly become the media darling. You can't open a newspaper or magazine, or flip on the radio or TV without coming across some reference to The Fortune Man."

"And to think that everyone—me included—predicted that when Taylor Fortune took over the company, it would crumble around him within the year. I know his brothers were all worried. Especially when he decided to market that robot."

"So now all they have to worry about is Taylor getting hitched."

"The guy would have to be out of his mind to get married and give up everything. He's sitting on top of a gold mine...."

"Has any woman he wants just for the asking...."

"He doesn't even have to ask."

"I've got to give him credit. He's pulled off the advertising coup of a lifetime."

"Hey, give credit where credit is due. This whole campaign was the brainchild of Ali Spencer. I wouldn't mind hiring her myself to do some marketing for my company."

"The line forms on the right. And it goes clear around the block. Everyone and his brother wants to be Spencer's client."

"The word's out that she's so hot she's opening her own agency. I bet she's sitting on cloud nine."

ACTUALLY, AT THAT PRECISE moment, Ali was sitting at her kitchen table staring glumly down at an evening edition of the *Denver Chronicle*. Sara, recuperating from a head cold, shuffled in with a mug of tea and glanced down over Ali's shoulder.

"Good photo. But he looks better in person. Who's the broad with him?" Sara quipped.

Ali shrugged. "Some debutante. Tomorrow, I'm sure there'll be photos of him with Lilli Wells. They went to a party together tonight. And tomorrow night he's off to cut the ribbon on a new wing at Denver General Hospital. I'm sure the photographers will snap him being surrounded by a bevy of luscious candy stripers." She shrugged again. "Publicity's booming. I just hope he can keep it up," she replied sardonically.

Sara slid into a seat across from her roommate, watching her fold the paper and set it aside. She knew it was Ali's way of saying, "Discussion closed." "So, did you finalize things with Chester today?"

Ali nodded. "I agreed to stay on another couple of weeks to tie up loose ends and help him interview for the publicist who'll take my place. He's actually been very nice about it. Everyone's been very nice. I've got a stack of 'Best Wishes' cards on my desk. I even got a bouquet of roses today from Steve Dennis, wishing me well in my new digs."

"Do you think he's angling for a spot in your new agency? Or in your bed?"

Ali gave her a droll look. "Knowing Dennis, I'd say probably both."

Sara grinned. "And knowing you, I'd say he's wasting his time. On both counts."

"You'd be right."

"Not that Steve Dennis is a total loser. Okay, he's no Fortune Man. . . ."

Ali gave Sara a sharp look. "Don't start."

Sara proffered an innocent smile. "What am I starting? I only said—"

"I don't want to talk about Taylor Fortune."

"I was talking about Steve Dennis."

"Did you see him on that TV talk show the other night?"

"Steve Dennis?"

Ali ignored Sara's question. "And here he is, the man of the hour, that inimitable mix of brains, style and dashing good looks—ladies and gentlemen, I give you The Fortune Man. . . ."

Sara grinned. Ali's imitation of the local late-night talk-show host, Lee Vincent, was excellent.

"And Taylor didn't disappoint Vincent's audience or his millions of TV viewers. With that roguish smile, the slicked-down hair, the velvet-sandpaper drawl, he was positively entrancing. I'm sure that by the next morning, Fortune's cash registers all over the Northwest were working overtime."

"Well," Sara said, "isn't that the point?"

But Ali wasn't listening. "And did you see the way he rolled up his shirtsleeves when Vincent brought on that beauty-contest winner, Miss You-Can-Have-Me?"

"I believe that was Miss Yukon. Or maybe that was what they called her for short," Sara quipped.

The remark went ignored. Ali was still on her own track. "He did it purely for effect. He's been working out and he happens to have extremely muscular forearms. Which Miss You-Make-Me-Sick was certainly quick to notice. By the end of the hour she was practically drooling over him."

"If I didn't know better," Sara said with a sly smile, "I'd say you were jealous, Ali Spencer."

Ali gave her roommate an indignant look. "Jealous? Me? Certainly not. I'm thrilled. I couldn't be more thrilled. Thanks to Taylor's . . . forearms, I'm about to open my own agency. With a client list that would make anyone . . ."

Sara eyed her over the rim of her teacup. "Drool."

Ali bristled. "I just think Taylor's overdoing it a little. I'm even beginning to wonder if it's even an act anymore." She gave Sara a wan look. "He's become such a smooth operator with his grab bag of smiles, his glib lines, his slick, superficial charm. And he seems so damn proud of his accomplishments. Every time I see him lately, he's just so—so full of himself. I think he actually expects me to pin some kind of a damn medal on him. I started out feeling like Professor Higgins, and now I feel more like Dr. Frankenstein."

Sara rose and patted Ali sympathetically on the shoulder. "I guess, for it all, the once-naive, goofy, awkward Taylor Fortune did have a certain charm."

Ali found herself smiling wistfully. "I guess he did."

THE NEXT DAY, SHORTLY before noon, just as Ali was in the middle of exercising to a Jane Fonda workout tape, Taylor showed up at her door. He was casually dressed in a charcoal silk shirt and white chinos, the creases at the corners of his eyes deepening as he smiled at her.

"You stood me up."

She gave him a blank look, blotting the sweat from her face with the back of her hand and then absently smoothing down the long white shirt that she'd thrown over her skimpy leotard.

"Say, that shirt looks familiar," Taylor murmured as he stepped inside her apartment.

Ali flushed. She was wearing Taylor's shirt—the one she'd borrowed after their wild, crazy, romantic tryst on the island. "Oh. I meant to . . . return it."

He smiled. "No. Keep it. It looks much better on you."

"No. Really, I . . ." She started to slip it off, but when she saw Taylor's eyes dart to the snug little black leotard barely covering her body, she thought better of it, quickly buttoning the shirt up. "I'll have it laundered—"

A mischievous smile tilted the corners of his mouth. "No. Don't do that."

Ali felt a flash of irritation at the flirtatious intent of his remark. "Save it for your fan club, Taylor. And what do you mean, I stood you up?"

"We had a strategy meeting planned for eleven this morning. You were supposed to meet me at the Café Museo."

"I left you a message yesterday that I . . . couldn't make it."

He stepped closer to her. "You're sweating."

"I was . . . working out."

He stared down into her face. "You've been avoiding me lately, Ali."

His intense scrutiny made her uneasy. "We've both been very busy. Our schedules just haven't ... meshed."

"I thought you were going to meet me after my appearance on the Lee Vincent show the other night."

"Something came up."

"Then you didn't catch the show?"

She looked away. "No," she lied.

Taylor felt a stab of disappointment. "Oh, that's too bad. You would have been real proud of me."

"I'm sure you were fantastic."

"Vincent invited me to come back on the show in a couple of weeks. And bring Homer." As he spoke, he nonchalantly began rolling up the cuffs of his shirtsleeves. As Ali stared at his tanned, muscular forearms, her lips curled.

"And I bet Miss Yukon invited you to come back to her apartment. Without Homer."

He lifted an eyebrow. "So you did see the show."

Ali reddened and turned away from Taylor. "I just caught a few minutes of it. Look, I need to take a shower and get dressed. I'm sorry about the meeting today, but—"

His hand shot out and caught hold of her arm, pulling her back around to face him. "I don't get it, Ali. Aren't you pleased? Isn't this what you wanted?"

A small pulse began to throb in her throat. Her mouth felt dry. Erotic memories flickered unbidden through her mind as she felt the pressure of his grip. She had to use every ounce of will to meet his gaze. And when she did, confusion mixed with desire. He had changed so much. He wore his veneer of superficial allure like a second skin now. Or maybe it wasn't merely skin-deep anymore. He seemed positively thrilled with his new persona. He seemed perfectly at ease being the center of attention these days. Glamorous women were falling over him left and right and he was handling them all with aplomb. Maybe, Ali silently rued, she had taught him too well....

"It seems to me we both have what we want, Taylor," she said, trying to keep her expression cool and guarded, determined not to reveal anything of what she was thinking.

Taylor was utterly baffled by Ali's aloof manner. He sensed her disapproval and disappointment with him and he couldn't figure it out. Wasn't he finally everything she'd wanted him to be? How come he'd been so irresistible to her when he was all-thumbs, and now she was avoiding him like the plague? Or had she just felt sorry for him? Had she made love to him out of pity? Or to inspire him with the confidence he needed to be The Fortune Man? He felt a wave of despair. Didn't she know that she was constantly on his mind, that just hearing her voice on the phone drove him to distraction, that being here with her now made him ache with desire? Maybe, he thought, he still wasn't slick enough. Maybe it was time to turn on the charm where it really counted.

With a boldness that wasn't easy to muster, he loosened his hold on her arm, and let his hand skim lightly up her sleeve across her shoulder to her neck. "Miss Yukon did invite me up to her apartment, but I turned her down. She isn't my type."

Ali, taken aback both by Taylor's seductive maneuver and his suggestive remark, gave him a dazed look.

"I'm afraid," Taylor murmured, gently scraping her cheek with the back of his knuckles, "I'm just a sucker for corkscrew curls and freckles."

Ali blinked several times. "Are you...coming on me, Taylor?" The words seemed to have left her mouth of their own volition.

In answer, he slipped his arm around her shoulders and pulled her body close to his. She started to pull away, disturbed by the look of challenge in his eyes and the stubborn set of his jaw, but Taylor's hold on her was firm.

"Taylor, I don't think—"

"Don't think." He closed a handful of her curls in his fist. Ali felt dizzy, as if she were being catapulted to the edge of a cliff.

Again she opened her mouth to protest, but this time his mouth swooped down over hers. Her lips parted involuntarily, but when their tongues tangled, a wave of desire curled through her. She felt starved for the touch and taste of him. She longed to give in fully to her yearning. And yet something held her back. Taylor's new brashness and arrogance made her uneasy, wary. She didn't trust the new Taylor. She wasn't so sure she even liked him.

Taylor could feel her resistance, but it only made him feel determined to try harder. He deepened the kiss, moving his hand boldly under her shirt to the leotard that hugged her body like a second skin. His palm slid sinuously up her rib cage and cupped her breast through the clingy cotton/Lycra fabric. "Oh, Ali, you feel so good. I've missed this. I know that we agreed to keep it strictly business, but I want you so much. And you want me, too."

It was true. She did. But he seemed so sure of himself, so smooth. *Too* smooth.

"Taylor, I don't—"

"You're a lousy liar." He prayed that he was right as he began unbuttoning her shirt.

She rushed to rebutton it, trying to hold her ground. "I've got to take a shower...."

"I guess that's one way of laundering my shirt," he said with a sly smile as she finished doing up the last button.

"Very amusing."

His expression sobered. "I haven't had many complaints."

"I'm sure you haven't," she retorted.

He expelled a frustrated sigh. "But I can't seem to please you."

"Well, I'm sorry to break your track record," she retorted.

Just then, something snapped in Taylor. It had been building for weeks. All the strain of his charade, of seeing Ali moving farther and farther away from him, of feeling like he was trapped on a Ferris wheel that was spinning out of control.

"You need a shower, all right," he muttered. And before Ali knew what was happening, he'd scooped her up in his arms and started marching down the hall.

"What are you doing? Put me down." She flailed her arms and legs, feeling much the way she had when that insufferable robot had captured her in its steel grip. But this was worse. This wasn't some mechanical monster manhandling her. This was Taylor. What had come over him? Who did he think he was? *The Fortune Man, that's who,* a tiny voice in her head answered.

Sara, hearing the commotion, stuck her head out of her bedroom. With a broad grin, she ducked back into her room before she was spotted. Then she grabbed a sweater and her purse, and as soon as the pair was out of sight, she slipped out of her room and out of the apartment. Just before she shut the front door, she called out, "Have fun, Ali. I'll be back tonight."

Ali grimaced. She had just been about to tell Taylor that he had to behave himself because her roommate was home.

Taylor pressed her against the bathroom door as he gripped the knob and swung the door open.

"Okay, now you can just put me down and go home," she said tightly.

Taylor put her down. But instead of making a gentlemanly exit, he brazenly reached behind him and locked the door. "Turn on the water."

Ali stared at him defiantly. "If you think I'm going to get undressed and get into that shower—"

"You don't want to get undressed? Fine." He brushed past her in the tight confines of the bathroom and turned the shower on himself.

Ali made a dash for the door, her fingers fumbling with the lock. Before she managed to turn it, she once again found herself in Taylor's firm embrace, her feet a good six inches off the ground.

"I think we both need to cool off," Taylor murmured.

"Oh, no," Ali protested. "Do you remember the last time you said that? We both ended up naked and—"

"Okay, we'll just keep our clothes on, then, if you don't think you can control yourself—"

"What are you . . . ?"

Taylor kicked off his shoes, and then, with Ali still gathered in his arms, he stepped into the shower. They both gasped as the water gushed down over them.

"Taylor, that's a silk shirt you're wearing," Ali sputtered. "You'll ruin it."

"This was your idea."

"My idea? Why, I . . . I . . ."

"Soap?"

She looked at his extended hand holding a bar of soap, then at his drenched clothes, and finally up at his face, with water streaming down it. Then she burst into laughter. "You're crazy. Do you know that?"

"And you've got a great laugh. Do you know that?"

She stopped laughing. "You always seem to say the right thing these days."

Taylor looked at her, nonplussed. "You think I'm handing you a line?"

"I'm not sure what you're doing," she said, shivering. "The water's cold."

"I can make it hotter," he replied, amusement lurking at the corners of his mouth as he leaned toward her, moving his hand around her to adjust the water temperature. Then his hand found its way to the buttons of her shirt again. "The shirt looks laundered now, Ali. I think you can take it off."

Ali was sorely tempted. She could no more deny that she wanted Taylor than that she was soaking wet. But this wasn't the Taylor she wanted. This Taylor seemed too sure of himself, too much the seducer. She longed for the old Taylor—the sweet, endearing, honest, awkward Taylor. But that Taylor seemed all but obliterated.

She pressed her palms against his chest. "I can't do this." And then, before he could say or do anything, she rushed out of the shower, quickly unlocked the bathroom door, and, dripping wet, raced out of the bathroom.

"Ali!" Taylor called out, chasing after her.

He had almost caught up to her when the doorbell rang. Ali dashed to the door, with Taylor in pursuit. Just as she flung the door open, Taylor slid on a wet spot on the wooden floor, let out a yelp of surprise and started to go down. Ali reached out to try to break his fall, only to end up landing on top of him on the floor.

Jessica Fortune and Ben Engel stood at the open door and stared down at the soaked, disheveled pair with amused expressions. Then Jessica turned to Ben. "It must be raining. Pity we didn't think to bring our umbrella."

Mortified, Ali struggled to her feet, urging Taylor to get up with her. "We were . . . fixing the . . . shower. I was trying . . . to fix it. And then Taylor came over. And so, he . . . got in and . . . tried. And then . . ." As she stammered she kept pushing her dripping ringlets off her face.

"You got it fixed?" Jessica offered.

Taylor grinned, combing his wet hair back with his fingers. "It's still not working perfectly."

Ben's eyes sparkled. "We've obviously caught you at a bad moment."

"Yes, we won't keep you," Jessica said. "It's just that a special-delivery letter came for you this morning, Taylor. I signed for it since you weren't at home. I thought it might be important. So, we took the chance that you might be over here."

Jessica slipped the envelope out of her purse and extended it to Taylor. He wiped his hands on his trousers, which didn't help to dry them much.

"I'll get you a towel," Ali said.

Taylor looked at his grandmother. "You open it."

"Perhaps," Ben suggested, "I should wait down in the lobby."

"No," Taylor said with a smile. "You're practically one of the family, Ben."

Both Ben and Jessica blushed.

"Go on, Gran. What does it say?" Taylor asked as he looked at Ali and held her gaze.

Jessica read the brief note through to herself and then chuckled. "Well, Taylor, you're certainly becoming quite the celebrity. You've been asked to cohost this year's Miss International beauty contest. Why, I believe the show is televised by satellite all over the world."

Taylor gave his grandmother a flabbergasted look. "Cohost a beauty contest?"

Jessica smiled. "I wonder if you'll have to sing. You know, when the winner walks down the runway, the tears streaming down her face as she blows kisses—"

"Sing? I can't . . ." Taylor turned a suspicious gaze on Ali. "This wasn't your doing?"

"Hey, look," she said defensively, "you didn't have any trouble with Miss Yukon the other night."

"That's not the same thing," Taylor countered.

"I thought it would be fabulous PR for Fortune's. A chance for you to spread into an international market. The publicity will bring in an avalanche of orders for Homer. I expected you to be thrilled."

"It is a wonderful opportunity, Taylor," Jessica said, but before she could say anything more, Ben nudged her. Jessica nodded, placing the special-delivery letter on the hall table. "Well, we'll leave you two to dry off and discuss the matter." She started to close the door. "Oh, one more thing. I'm having a little dinner party tomorrow night and I'd like you both to come. Eight o'clock. See you then."

Ali and Taylor stared at the closed door, then back at each other.

"We should get out of these wet clothes," she muttered. "You can have your jeans back that I borrowed...."

Taylor picked up the letter. "It's in New York. I'm supposed to be there in two weeks."

"If you really don't think you can handle it, Taylor..." She looked at him, stunned to realize just how desperately she wanted him to say that he'd be too uncomfortable, too nervous to go through with it. It would mean that he hadn't really changed as much as she'd feared. It stunned her to realize that seeing Taylor as his old self again was more important to her than her whole career. So, she thought, humbled, this was what love was all about.

Little did Ali guess that the very thought of cohosting a beauty pageant filled Taylor with despair and trepidation. All of those beauty contestants fawning over him, once again having to be in the spotlight, being expected to act charming and suave—Taylor still found it all overwhelming and terribly uncomfortable. But he knew how hard Ali had worked to get him this spot. It was a public-relations dream come true, bound to enhance and spread her reputation. There was no way he could back out. Besides, he saw the challenging look in her face. Was she still afraid he would let her down? Did she still doubt that he would come through for her? He took in a resigned breath. If she wanted The Fortune Man, that's just what she would get.

His mouth curled in a cocky grin that he'd practiced in front of a mirror for weeks. "Well, I've got two weeks to learn how to sing."

11

ALI KNEW SOMETHING was up the minute Taylor arrived the next evening to take her to dinner at Jessica's. For one thing, he was a half hour early. For another, he seemed nervous, agitated. Ali felt a flurry of hope. Had he decided he didn't want to cohost the beauty pageant, after all? Was he anxious about admitting it, afraid he'd disappoint her? Oh, she thought, if only he knew how relieved she'd be.

"Come in, Taylor. I'm almost ready."

He stepped inside the apartment, but lingered by the door.

"How about a drink while you're waiting?"

"No. Thanks. I . . . don't want . . ."

Ali looked at him encouragingly. "You don't want . . . ?"

"A . . . drink." He quirked an uneasy smile. "I'm afraid liquor still . . . goes to my head."

She smiled, remembering, as she knew he was, that first evening up at Fortune's when they'd feasted on caviar and got drunk on champagne. A little laugh escaped her lips as she thought about Taylor's distressed phone call the next morning after discovering he'd arrived home the night before without his trousers. It almost brought tears to her eyes, recalling his sweet innocence and mortification at the thought that he might have behaved in a less-than-gentlemanly fashion.

"Sorry. I didn't mean to laugh." She reached out and lightly touched his arm. "How about lemonade?"

Taylor's eyes fell on her hand, which was still on his arm. "Ali."

"Yes, Taylor?"

There was a pregnant silence.

Oh, poor Taylor, Ali thought. *He's finding this so hard.* If only she could make it easier for him.

"You look a little tired, Taylor. You've been on quite a merry-go-round these past few weeks. I guess I didn't realize that being The Fortune Man would capture so much of your time and energy. Now that things are going so well, it probably wouldn't matter if you took some time off. Even got away for a while. You could even use my cottage. Just take it easy for a few weeks—swim, hike, relax. Even The Fortune Man needs a break. You really don't want to push yourself too hard, too fast. You don't have to do anything you don't want to do. Some things just might not be right for you. And that's okay. I mean...anyone would understand. Me, most of all."

Taylor adjusted his silk paisley tie. "Ali."

"Yes, Taylor?"

Again there was a pause, as Taylor shifted his weight from one foot to the other. Ali decided he'd feel more at ease sitting down.

"Come on into the living room and relax for a few minutes, Taylor. All I have to do is find my pumps and run a comb through my hair. We have a few minutes just to... chat."

She took his arm, but Taylor didn't budge.

"Maybe you're right, Ali."

"I am?" And then, quickly, reassuringly, "Oh, I am right, Taylor. Believe me, in this business you have to be sensitive to a client's needs, know what's best for him—"

"Thanks, Ali. A glass of lemonade will hit the spot."

"Lemonade?" She stared at him blandly. "Oh, you mean...to drink. Right. Oh, yes. Lemonade. Just the thing for you. Just what I thought you needed."

He followed her into the kitchen. She opened the fridge. A few moments later she glanced over her shoulder and smiled sheepishly. "I'm afraid Sara must have finished the lemonade. Will . . . orange juice do?"

He crossed the room like a man with a mission, pulling Ali away from the fridge and shutting the door. "I really shouldn't stay. I mean...I should come back. Or I could send Daniel over...."

Ali scowled. "I don't understand, Taylor."

"There's a woman—"

"A woman?"

"Waiting in my car."

Ali stared at him with a dazed look. "There's a woman waiting in your car?"

He nodded.

"She's waiting for you?"

"Well . . . yes."

Ali was stunned. "You mean you have another date for the evening."

"Not exactly. But, of course, I invited her to join us. You and me. And the whole family. For dinner at my grandmother's. I mean . . . it was the only proper thing to do. It's Fiona Jordan."

Ali gave him a blank look.

"Miss International, 1988. From Great Britain."

"You certainly do seem to attract your share of beauty queens, Taylor."

"She's an actress now. On the London stage. And she's my cohost. For this year's Miss International contest. She was in Denver on business and she had some spare time. So she thought it would be a good idea for us to . . . get acquainted before we started formal rehearsals in New York. You know . . . break the ice."

Ali smiled sarcastically. "Yes. Break the ice."

They stared at each other in awkward silence.

Taylor cleared his throat. "Orange juice would be...fine."

Ali made no move.

"Or maybe I should pop downstairs and tell Fiona—"

Before he finished the sentence the doorbell rang. They shared a look.

Taylor smiled uneasily. "That might be—"

"Fiona?"

They walked to the front door together, Ali very conscious now of being barefoot and not even having her hair combed. She felt even more conscious of her appearance after she opened the door.

In her silver ankle-strapped stiletto heels, Fiona Jordan stood close to six feet tall, an exquisite amazon with a thick mane of stick-straight wheat-colored hair with creamy natural-blond flashes falling to her shoulders. It was the kind of hair Ali had always craved. Not that Fiona's hair was all that Ali found enviable. The ex-beauty queen cum actress was a knockout—from her perfectly coiffed head to her perfectly manicured toes.

Besides looking ravishing, she looked a little bored and, when her gaze fell on Ali, a little condescending. Not that Fiona wasted much time looking at her.

Dismissing her after a brief glance, Fiona smiled petulantly at Taylor, flashing perfect white teeth. "I'm afraid I've never been very good at waiting, love."

Taylor smiled apologetically. "I'm sorry, Fiona. Ali just needs to . . . comb her hair and put her shoes on."

Right, Ali thought contemptuously. *And throw a potato sack over my head.*

"WHAT A CHARMING HOME, Mrs. Fortune," Fiona said in her clipped British accent. "It was so kind of you to invite me to your family dinner. I'm eager to meet the other famous Fortune boys. Oh, and their wives," she added offhandedly, slipping an arm through Taylor's, effectively separating him from his publicist. "Actually," she said in a breathy, affected voice, turning to him with an alluring smile, "I had the most marvelous idea. I think we should have all of your brothers make a brief appearance on the show. What if they served as escorts for the three runners-up? I'm sure Don Peters will go for the idea."

Taylor, acutely aware of how Fiona had wedged herself in between him and Ali, gave her a disconcerted look. "Don Peters?"

"The director, darling. Oh, and a former fiancé of mine. Thank heavens we both realized before we'd gone and done the dirty deed that neither of us was the marrying kind." She smiled coyly at Taylor. "Something the two of us have in common, love. Of course, I don't have a tontine to keep me in line."

Jessica watched Ali, who was looking as if steam were coming out of her ears as she glared venomously at Fiona. Yes, Jessica thought with delight, all the signs were there. If only the dear girl wouldn't fight it so hard. And Taylor, too. Perhaps Fiona Jordan's unexpected arrival would be just the spark to light the fire under those two. She only hoped it wouldn't set off the wrong kind of explosion.

"Don is a love, though," Fiona went on. "You'll adore working with him, darling. And he thinks you're simply divine. But then, don't we all?" As she tossed out the rhetorical question, her gaze remained fixed on Taylor.

Ali shot Jessica a wry smile. "Yes, don't we?"

Jessica rolled her eyes. "I think drinks are in order. Shall we adjourn to the parlor?"

Ali walked along with Jessica, Taylor and Fiona following behind.

"You wouldn't have any lemonade on hand, Jessica?" Ali asked, with a quick glance back at Taylor. "You know what happens to your grandson when he drinks."

Fiona arched a well-shaped blond eyebrow, a trace of hauteur in her gray-green eyes. "What *does* happen to you, Taylor?"

"He gets the urge to play his bagpipes," Ali deadpanned.

FIONA JORDAN HELD COURT at dinner. By the second course she appeared to have all the Fortune brothers eating out of her hand instead of their dinner plates. The women at the table, however, were less than entranced by the surprise addition to the menu.

"I mean it," Fiona was drawling British-style, looking from Adam to Tru to Peter and then resting her bedroom eyes on Taylor. "It would make a wonderful piece of theater. A play about the four fabulous Fortune brothers. What drama, what excitement, what romance, what angst!"

"What drivel," Eve muttered in a low voice that only her husband, Adam, heard. He gave her a disapproving look and then turned back to the ex-beauty queen.

"Tell me more about this idea of yours to have us on the Miss International show, Fiona."

Both Peter and Tru nodded, clearly intrigued by the prospect.

Fiona beamed. "I think it would be the perfect finale. A chance for the audience and the millions of telly viewers in the four corners of the globe to see all four fabulous Fortune brothers together onstage, surrounded by the most beautiful women in the world."

"Don't you think," Jessica commented lightly, "that all those viewers would also love to meet the women who stole the hearts of the—uh—fabulous foursome? I think it would be so dramatic. So . . . romantic."

There was an arrogant tilt to Fiona's sculptured chin as she turned to Jessica. "Don't you mean the *threesome?*"

Ali and Taylor flashed each other awkward looks.

Jessica batted her eyes. "Oh, isn't that what I said?"

Ben had to fight back a laugh.

"I think that's a great idea, Jessica," Eve was quick to say, and Elizabeth and Sasha seconded the suggestion.

"Tru and I are to be returning to New York anyway, so this would be an excellent idea," Sasha said enthusiastically. "And I think it would be most exciting to appear on American television. Just think, Tru, our friends in Russia will be able to see us. It will be good publicity, yes?"

Tru had to agree.

"Good publicity for all the Fortunes," Elizabeth pointed out. "Plus, Peter's been thinking about exploring the possibility of opening a new haberdashery branch in Manhattan, and I've got a month's vacation coming."

"We could shop, see some plays, go to the Met," Eve said excitedly.

"And top it off with an appearance on the Miss International show," Elizabeth added.

Fiona gave Elizabeth a dubious look. "Well, I don't know that Don would go along with it."

Taylor, buoyed by the thought of his whole family being there with him—for him—onstage, plucked an irrepressible smile from his grab bag and served it up to his cohost. "I'm sure you can be very persuasive when you want to be, Fiona. Especially with someone you were so close to at one time."

"Well," Fiona murmured, her eyes fixed on Taylor, "I'll give it my best shot, love."

Jessica snuck a smile at Ben. "Why don't we all go?" She saw Fiona blanch, and laughed. "Oh, don't worry. Ben and I don't want to appear onstage. Especially not with a bevy of young beauties. I'd feel depressingly old. And Ben might forget how old he is."

Ben chuckled. But then he gently touched Jessica's cheek. "You'd put those young whippersnappers to shame, Jess."

Jessica smiled. "Will you come with us to New York, Ben?"

"I haven't been to New York in a long time," he mused. "It sounds like a good idea."

"It's the perfect place for a vacation," Eve remarked.

Ben winked at Jessica. "Yes, a perfect place for a vacation or . . . whatever."

Jessica blushed, then quickly shifted her gaze to Ali, who had remained very quiet during the whole discussion of the jaunt to New York. "You must come, too, my dear."

"Oh, no, I...couldn't," Ali muttered, but then she caught the glint of satisfaction in Fiona's eyes. And was that a flash of disappointment in Taylor's eyes? Or just wish fulfillment on her part? "Then again, I was planning a break before opening my new agency."

"You've got to come, Ali," Elizabeth said firmly. "You arranged the whole thing. You should be there to orchestrate the publicity there'll be from Taylor's appearance as the host of a beauty-queen pageant. You can't let an opportunity like this pass Fortune's by. Can she, Taylor?"

Taylor's gaze fixed on Ali. "No. No, she can't."

"Besides," Eve added when Ali made no response, "you're the only native New Yorker among us. You could show us all the real New York. Why, Taylor, you've never been to New York, have you? You've got to see the Statue of Liberty, the Empire State Building, the World Trade Center. . . ."

"I'm afraid Taylor won't have much time for sight-seeing," Fiona interrupted. "He and I are going to be incredibly busy rehearsing. I wouldn't be surprised if we were at it around the clock." She reached over to Taylor and squeezed his muscular forearm. Ali, sitting across from Fiona, could almost hear her purr with delight. "But don't worry," the ex-beauty queen murmured suggestively. "I'll look after The Fortune Man, and Ali can take care of the rest of you."

Ali's lips curled in a saccharine smile. "You mean you'll look after The Fortune Man and Homer."

Fiona squinted. "Homer?"

Taylor gave Ali a puzzled look, but then he broke into a wide grin. "Oh, absolutely. I'm sure Don will love the idea of having my robot make an appearance. He could even crown the new Miss International. It would be quite a novelty."

Jessica, who was sitting beside Ali, patted her hand affectionately. "What a brilliant promotion tactic. This will surely put the sales of the robots right over the top." She wagged a finger at Taylor. "This gal is something, my boy. You had better not let her get away."

Again Taylor's gaze fixed on Ali, but he didn't say a word. Ali stared uneasily down at her barely touched plate of smoked salmon. An awkward silence fell around the table. Even Fiona Jordan couldn't come up with an attention-getting remark.

In the end, it was Jessica who stole the limelight. After dinner, when everyone had gathered in the parlor, she calmly announced that there was to be another Fortune wedding.

Ali shot Taylor a look.

Taylor shot Ali a look.

Jessica laughed softly. "No, this time I am not the matchmaker." Her eyes sparkled as she paused and reached out her hand to Ben. He took her hand gently in his and brought it to his lips.

"This time," Jessica murmured, a rosy hue coloring her cheeks, "I am the bride."

For several moments, the stunned group remained motionless, expressionless. Jessica smiled shakily and Ben put his arm around her in a gesture that was part protective, part adoring.

"I want you all to know," Ben said solemnly, his voice gravelly with emotion, "that I love your grandmother dearly, and other than each other's love, there is nothing we want more than all of your blessings."

In one joined voice, the small group cheered. Even Fiona Jordan shed a tear and declared that this was the true stuff of theater. After all the grandchildren had hugged the newly engaged pair, Ali took her turn.

Jessica squeezed her tightly. "Something tells me this won't be the last Fortune wedding," she whispered in Ali's ear. When Ali stepped back, her lips held a wistful but dubious smile. The smile quickly disappeared as she turned to see Fiona throwing her arms around Taylor to congratulate him. What was worse was Taylor's response to the ex-beauty queen. With all his newly acquired Fortune Man allure and confidence, he swept Fiona up in his arms and did a graceful twirl with her.

Eve, standing just behind Ali, muttered acerbically, "You'd think he was the happy groom."

"Not very likely," Ali mumbled, and stalked off.

JESSICA AND BEN WERE married ten days later in a quaint little church in Denver. It was a small, simple ceremony attended by family and a few close friends. The groom was very dashing in a double-breasted blue suit, and the bride looked enchanting in a pale pink silk dress. As the happy pair said their "I do's," there wasn't a dry eye in the house.

In the front pew, the three married Fortune boys all held hands with their wives, sharing dreamy, adoring glances. Taylor, sitting at the end of the pew, kept glancing back at Ali, who had slipped into a back pew after arriving at the church a few minutes late. This was the first he'd seen her since the

dinner party at which his grandmother had announced her
plans to marry Ben. The next day she'd taken off "on business" and he hadn't been able to get in touch with her. Not
that he'd had much time. Fiona Jordan had ended up staying
in Denver for close to a week and she'd effectively taken up
most of his time "getting acquainted," convincing him that
establishing a compatible, friendly relationship would go a
long way toward making their appearance on the Miss International show a success. Taylor felt he owed it to Ali to be
a success—although a week of wining, dining, and fending
off Fiona's advances had left him feeling drained and irritable—and, thanks to Ali's disappearance, abandoned.

The reception was held back at Jessica's house. At least, it
was hers for the time being. Although her son had left her the
vast estate in his will, Jessica had decided to turn the whole
property, the main house included, over to her grandsons and
move into Ben's charming little mountain cottage just outside Denver. Secretly, she hoped that eventually all four of
her grandsons would settle on the compound with their wives
and children. The main house could easily be divided into
two large, comfortable apartments. Then there was Tru's delightful cottage that had a lot of room for expansion, and
lastly, there was Taylor's carriage house, which was certainly spacious enough to accommodate a family—even with
Homer taking up a large part of the basement.

A small group of well-wishers gathered around the new-
lyweds in the parlor, as Adam offered a toast.

"May *fortune* always smile down on you both and may you
look as happy at one hundred as you do today."

Everyone joined in the toast and sipped their champagne.

Taylor came up behind Ali. "They do look happy, don't
they?" he murmured.

Ali didn't turn around. "Yes. Very happy."

"I missed you."

"I hear you were pretty busy. Rehearsing."

He slipped a hand around her forearm. "Let's go out to the garden."

"I don't think—"

"I haven't stopping thinking."

Ali flashed him a look. He smiled crookedly. "If we stay here, I'm liable to drink too much champagne and make a fool of myself."

Ali thought to herself, *If I go out to the garden with you, I'm liable to make a fool of myself.* But she went.

They left the house through the French doors that led to a terrazzoed patio, then down stone steps to a bright, colorful garden that had been tended with expert loving care.

"Won't your grandmother miss all this?" Ali mused as they walked side by side along a winding slate walk.

"No," he said quietly. "I don't think she'll miss any of it."

Ali nodded silently.

"Why did you take off like that?" he asked without further preamble.

"You're not my only client, Taylor," she said more defensively than she intended.

"No. I suppose that's true."

She gave him a sideways glance. "Besides, Fiona kept you occupied most of the time I was gone."

He angled her a seductive smile. "Keeping tabs on me?"

"It's pretty hard to open a newspaper or magazine and not know what you've been up to." She had promised herself to keep her jealousy under wraps, but she realized now how difficult that was going to be. Drawing herself up, she plastered on a phony smile. "Not that I'm complaining. All that press with Fiona got me several more top clients. So we both made out like bandits."

Taylor felt a flash of anger. How could Ali think that spending all that time with Fiona was anything but tedious, awkward and dreary? Didn't she realize how much it took out of him to maintain this ludicrous image of The Fortune Man?

"Right. We both got what we want." He gave her a stony look and stormed off.

Ali felt compelled to chase after him. "I don't know what your gripe is, Taylor Fortune. You wanted to sell your robot and I've helped you make Homer a household word. Okay, you weren't all that keen on becoming The Fortune Man at first, but you sure learned fast. And you certainly don't seem to have any complaints lately. Then again, why *should* you complain?"

She grabbed his arm just as he swung open the door of his carriage house. "Why, look at you, Taylor. You're every woman's fantasy. You're more polished than the finest sterling silver, you're oozing with self-assurance, you radiate animal magnetism. A whole mystique has been created around you. You know what you've got, Taylor? You've got . . . killer charm. A month ago, a woman like Fiona Jordan would have laughed at your awkwardness, written you off with a dismissive glance as a nerd and hardly noticed you. But not anymore." She flung the compliments at him as if they were poisonous darts.

"And what about a woman like you, Ali?"

She was flustered by the question. Even more flustered when he took hold of her arm and pulled her inside the house. She was wearing a light pink organdy sundress and Taylor's hands pressed into her bare shoulders.

"Don't, Taylor." But her voice lacked conviction.

His fingers dug into her flesh. "Why does this killer charm I'm supposed to have leave you cold, Ali?"

"This isn't the time. . . . They'll miss us at the reception."

"You didn't miss me when I was a nerd. You made love with me, Ali."

"Taylor—"

"Oh, I was putty in your hands, all right. I was willing to go along with any scheme you had in mind."

Ali looked at him in astonishment. "You don't think . . . ?" Her expression turned to dark fury. "You actually think I slept with you to win the Fortune Man account?" She slapped him hard across the face.

He winced, tightening his grip on her for a moment, but then he let go of her, stepping back. There was a long pause and then he emitted a weary sigh. "I'm sorry, Ali. I don't really believe that. I just don't know what to think anymore. I don't know what it all means. All I know is I can't seem to get you out of my mind." He fixed her with his intense gaze. "When we made love, Ali, it was . . . every man's fantasy."

She tried to close her mind to what he was saying, his words resurrecting memories of passion and delight she'd been struggling for weeks to forget. She wanted to stay angry at him. That would be easier. Easier than this. "That's just what it was, Taylor," she whispered. "A fantasy. We'll both be a lot better off, leaving it at that."

"Will we?" he asked quietly, the look on his face so reminiscent of that sweet, awkward, naive fellow she'd talked into becoming The Fortune Man, that her heart lurched.

In the silence that followed, neither of them seemed able to summon the wherewithal to look away. And then, knowing full well that they were courting heartbreak, they moved as if magnetized into each other's arms.

His mouth descended in slow motion. Ali needed to tell him to stop, but the words wouldn't come. There was only desire. And then his warm lips touched hers. Instantly, her mouth opened to receive his tongue and they kissed with a bittersweet fervor, clinging hard, their hands stroking each other.

When they drew apart, their breathing was labored, their faces flushed.

"This isn't . . . right for us," she stammered.

He drew her closer, kissing her throat and jaw. "It feels right to me, Ali."

His hands were on the back zipper of her dress. Before she knew what was happening, it fell in a whoosh to the floor.

Next thing she knew, she was urgently divesting him of his tuxedo jacket, then popping open the little pearl buttons of his white pleated shirt. Somehow, she never got to the bow tie, even after they'd both stripped naked in record time.

She saw now that he was strikingly more muscular and tanned than before. And there wasn't even a tan line. Unlike the other intimate moments she'd shared with Taylor, this time Ali was a little in awe. This felt like the first time she was making love to The Fortune Man. She felt self-conscious, inhibited.

Not Taylor. Heady with the joy of being with her once again, he felt light-headed, giddy. This was what he wanted. This was where he longed to be. He didn't think of himself as The Fortune Man. He'd played the part and gotten quite good at it, but it had always been a strain and never felt like him. It never would.

He lifted her curls off her neck and planted kisses along her nape. He stroked her naked body, reveling in the silky feel of her.

Ali's inhibitions began to melt. A sense of lassitude stole over her as he eased her down onto the carpet. She searched his face until she saw the Taylor Fortune she knew and loved. Yes, *loved*.

"Oh, Taylor, Taylor, Taylor," she crooned as they rolled over and over on the carpet, knocking over a chair, banging up against a table. Her hair tangled with his, her long, creamy legs wrapped around his. When he entered her, she cried out. And when they reached climax, they both let out an uninhibited cry of satisfaction.

They were just beginning to melt into the afterglow when a voice behind them made them jump apart.

"This must be the most beautiful girl in the world. . . ."

Ali gasped in mortification, then spun around, red-faced, only to discover Homer with his happy, smiley face beaming down at her.

Taylor grinned sheepishly. "I've been programming him to give a little speech when he comes onstage with the crown for Miss International."

The interruption brought Ali sharply to her senses. She started to rise and grab for her dress, but Taylor caught hold of her, determined to use all of his Fortune Man charms to win her over. Giving her a killer smile, he murmured glibly, "If it were up to me, I'd crown you, Ali."

"Ditto," she muttered sarcastically.

It was at that moment that Ali truly felt like Dr. Frankenstein with a runaway monster. And her greatest wish was that she could somehow undo the damage she'd done to Taylor so that he could go back to being the sweet, decent, unassuming man he'd been before she started messing up his entire life. But Taylor seemed so pleased with his new Fortune Man persona. And so successful. She was afraid it was too late.

12

THE FORTUNE ENTOURAGE'S arrival in New York was accompanied by gushes of hype and hoopla. Everyone in the family got their share, but no one got more than Taylor—the celebrated Fortune Man. Taylor's appearance rivaled that of any screen idol or rock star, and began the moment he stepped off the jet at Kennedy. Waiting at the arrivals gate were hordes of paparazzi, flashbulbs exploding, and just beyond them, a throng of women of every age, shape, and size, all of whom, it seemed, were part of The Fortune Man fan club. There were screams and moans; several women swooned. They were waving welcome banners, photos, We Love Fortune's signs, scraps of paper and pens. Everyone wanted The Fortune Man's autograph. From the avaricious look on some of their faces, they wouldn't have minded locks of his hair, scraps of his clothing. Airport security guards trained in crowd control had all they could do to hold off the frantic fans and keep them behind the designated lines.

Taylor, awestruck and overcome by the media circus and the mobs of hysterical fans, hung back by the tunnel doors, tempted to make a run for it back to the jet. But Ali was behind him, blocking his escape.

"Was this your doing?" he asked anxiously.

Ali shook her head. "This kind of thing can snowball. I may have started the ball rolling, but at this point it's bigger than both of us. You're the flavor of the month, Taylor."

"The ... what?"

She smiled crookedly. "It's a show-biz term. You're hot, kid. A media darling. You've heard of the Gold Rush. Well, this is the Fortune Rush."

Jessica, Ben, his three brothers and their wives all glanced back, eyeing the man of the moment with a mix of sympathy and envy.

Ali gave him a little nudge. "Come on. They won't bite." And then, surveying the screeching crowd, she amended, "Or maybe they will."

Just after Taylor finished taking a deep breath to steel himself for the trek across the terminal to the exit doors, a tall, svelte blonde in a clinging peacock blue mid-thigh jersey shift, surrounded by her own small entourage, broke through the swarms. Another round of flashbulbs began furiously popping and there were more screams and shrieks from the crowd as the ex-beauty queen cum actress, Fiona Jordan, was recognized. The noise level reached a fever pitch as she headed straight for Taylor, who was blinded by all the flashbulbs. With a cry of delight, she threw her arms around his neck and kissed him with Oscar-winning ardor.

There was nothing for Ali or the rest of the Fortune clan to do but watch. As for Taylor, he was too dumbstruck by his cohost's surprise assault to do much of anything but stand there and take it.

"Darling," Fiona gushed as she reluctantly pried her mouth from his. "Isn't this a grand reception?" She turned slightly to give the paparazzi a shot of her and Taylor cheek to cheek. "Smile, love," she muttered under her breath.

Taylor attempted a smile, and with some effort managed to disentangle himself from Fiona's clutches. "Fiona, you remember my publicist—" But when he turned to Ali, she was gone. He caught his grandmother's eye as she gestured with a nod toward the terminal exit.

Eve, meanwhile, gave Elizabeth and Sasha knowing looks and they made a beeline for Taylor, effectively edging the publicity-happy Fiona out of the way. "We should get out of here before there's a riot," Eve declared, gripping one of Taylor's arms firmly while Elizabeth latched on to the other. Then, with Sasha running interference up front and the help of security guards, the whole Fortune entourage elbowed their way through the crowd to the exit, Eve shouting whenever anyone got too close, "Please, I'm pregnant. Give us some room!"

Two stretch limos were waiting to take them to suites at the posh Plaza Hotel in midtown Manhattan. Taylor hoped to find Ali waiting in one of the cars, but no such luck. He felt abandoned and still in shock—not only from the unexpected and frenetic welcoming party, but from Fiona Jordan's amorous greeting.

He got into the first limo with Adam and Eve, and Elizabeth and Peter. Jessica, Ben, Sasha and Tru filed into the second one.

Eve, who slid in beside Taylor, slipped a tissue from her purse and wiped Fiona's bright red lipstick off his lips.

Taylor scowled. "I know that kiss was ninety percent hype, but I can't say that I appreciate being...used in that way."

Adam grinned. "You wouldn't find too many men complaining if they were in your shoes, Taylor."

"I know just how Taylor feels," Eve countered. "Like a—"

Elizabeth supplied the rest: "Sex object."

"Exactly," Taylor said, so emphatically everyone laughed. Everyone but Taylor.

After the laughter died down, Taylor asked if any of them knew what had happened to Ali.

"I heard her mumble something about checking on the crate you shipped Homer in," Peter said.

Taylor rolled his eyes. "Homer. I forgot all about him."

Adam chuckled. "Well, if I were a sex object for the likes of Fiona Jordan, I'd forget about robots, too," he teased.

Eve jabbed him in the ribs and he smiled contritely.

Peter rubbed his palms together. "I've got to hand it to you, Taylor. And Ali. You two put everything you had, and some extra that none of us knew you had, into this Fortune Man campaign and it's paying off in spades. None of us was able to do what you've done with Fortune's, Taylor. Sales have never been better and this is only the beginning. We're all really proud of you."

Adam was quick to offer his congratulations, as well. "I wonder," he mused, "if Dad ever dreamed that the little company he started nearly fifty years ago would one day have a celebrated international reputation."

"I wonder," mused Elizabeth, "if your dad ever dreamed that even with his tontine, three of his sons would choose marriage over Fortune's."

"And you know the old saying," Eve interjected with a mischievous smile. "The count's not over until the fat lady sings."

Adam gave Taylor an edgy look. "I'll confess we were all a little worried for a time that you and Ali . . ." He squirmed under his kid brother's scrutiny.

Peter felt obliged to pinch-hit. "It's obvious the two of you have some real feelings for each other, Taylor, but I think you both have had enough sense to realize . . ." Now he looked to Adam for help.

Adam obliged. "To realize what was at stake." His features softened. "And thanks to you and Ali, there's more at stake now than ever. With any luck, Fortune's could become the number-one chain of upscale department stores in the country."

"Hey, after this Miss International pageant gets broadcast all over the globe," Pete interjected, "you could branch out in the European market without much sweat. You'll be golden, Taylor."

Taylor regarded his brothers with a rueful grimace. "Right. The man with the Midas touch. The flavor of the month. Every woman's impossible dream. The rich, alluring, cosmopolitan, charming, untouchable Fortune Man."

Eve and Elizabeth gazed sympathetically at Taylor. Then Eve eyed the two brothers. "It isn't fair, you know. Taylor's as entitled to love and marriage as the rest of you. If that's what he wants."

"It's different for Taylor, Eve," Adam countered. "If he marries—"

"Yes, I know," his wife cut him off. "The fabulously successful Fortune's chain goes to Nolan Fielding. It's the end of a family business. And I know that isn't an easy thing to give up—not to mention the enormous wealth and status that goes with it. But you, Pete and Tru gave it up for love. Why shouldn't Taylor—?"

"Look," Taylor retorted with surprising sharpness, "I'd appreciate it if you'd all stop discussing my love life. Not that there's much of it left to discuss. Ali told me while we were in flight that, after the pageant, she's dropping me."

"Dropping you as a client?" Peter queried.

Taylor gave him a weary look. "She thinks I'm finally slick enough, sophisticated enough, polished enough to carry on the campaign on my own. As she put it, there's nothing more I need. Or, at least, nothing more she thinks she can give me."

Eve scowled. "I don't believe that."

"Neither do I," Elizabeth seconded.

Taylor sighed. "The point is, Ali believes it."

Eve lifted an eyebrow. "I wonder."

PAPARAZZI AND FANS were waiting for Taylor at the Plaza Hotel. The one person he'd hoped would be waiting for him, however, was nowhere to be found. He locked himself up alone in his suite and dialed down to the front desk.

"Has Miss Ali Spencer checked in yet?" he asked the desk clerk.

"One moment, Mr. Fortune."

Taylor impatiently tapped his fingers on the phone, waiting for the clerk to get back on the line.

"I'm sorry, Mr. Fortune. Miss Spencer has canceled her rooms at the hotel."

"Canceled? What do you mean, she's canceled?" he demanded.

"I'm very sorry, Mr. Fortune," the desk clerk murmured obsequiously.

"Well, if she's not staying here, damn it, where is she staying?"

The desk clerk nervously cleared his throat. "I'm sorry, Mr. Fortune—"

"Will you stop saying, I'm sorry," he snapped, slamming the receiver down in the cradle.

A moment later, stunned and appalled by his rude outburst, Taylor dialed down to the desk again.

"I'm sorry," he said remorsefully to the desk clerk.

"That's all right, Mr. Fortune. I understand."

"Do you?"

"Why, yes, sir. A man of your prominence and stature—"

"What's your name?"

The desk clerk hesitated, no doubt fearing he would be reported. "My name's Carl, Mr. Fortune. Carl Weltman. If there's any way I can be of service to you, Mr. Fortune . . ."

Taylor stretched out on the blue velvet settee. "I'm in love, Carl."

"Sir?"

"With Miss Spencer. The vanished Miss Spencer. I'm in love with her, Carl."

"Yes, sir. I see...."

"You're actually the first one I've told, Carl."

"I'm...honored, sir."

"I haven't even told her. And certainly no one in my family."

"No, sir."

"It's this damn tontine. Do you know about the tontine, Carl?"

"Yes, sir. I imagine everyone knows, Mr. Fortune."

"Call me Taylor, Carl. I don't want to even hear the word *fortune* right now. The thing is, Carl, it isn't only the tontine. Do you know what's really keeping me and Ali apart?"

"No, Mr. For—Taylor."

"It's me. Not me, the real me, Carl. The me I've become. Which I haven't really become. But she thinks I have. And she thinks I like it. But I don't like it, Carl. Oh, everyone else seems to like it, though. They're all tickled pink. Not Ali, though. She doesn't seem to like it at all. But it's what she wanted. I did it all for her. Naturally she thinks I did it for Homer...."

"Homer?"

Taylor scowled and sat up. "Where is Homer?"

"Is he registered at the hotel?"

"Damn it, Carl. I think Ali's run off with Homer."

"Oh, no. She couldn't. She wouldn't. I mean...I don't know her, but if you're in love with her—"

There was a knock on Taylor's door. "Someone's here. Maybe it's Ali. Wish me luck, Carl."

"Good luck, Taylor," the desk clerk said warmly. "I mean that sincerely."

"It really helped talking to you, Carl. Thanks," Taylor said and then hung up, racing for the door.

It wasn't Ali at the door. It was a New York publicist who wanted him to pose for a Fortune Man calendar.

"Think of it," the young woman in a pale peach suit said eagerly. "You'd probably outsell *Sports Illustrated*'s swimsuit calendar. Twelve glorious, revealing shots of The Fortune Man, one for each month of the year...."

Taylor blanched, said a succinct "No," and showed her out the door. He then proceeded to phone every member of his family to see if any of them had heard from Ali. None of them had.

About an hour later, there was another knock on the door. This time Taylor judiciously checked the peephole. A tidy young man dressed in a blue suit, white shirt and blue tie stood outside the door at attention. Behind him were two burly men in T-shirts, holding a large crate.

Taylor opened the door, hoping that the men were merely blocking Ali from view. His hopes were dashed.

The young man introduced himself as Carl. Taylor shook his hand and motioned for the deliverymen to carry in the crate.

Carl hesitated at the doorway and gestured toward the crate. "It made some . . . funny noises in the elevator."

Taylor laughed softly. "It's just Homer babbling. Probably practicing his speech for the Miss International pageant."

Carl blinked several times. "In a crate?"

"I'll end up having to take him apart again."

Carl turned white as Taylor walked over to the deliverymen and handed them a large tip before they left.

Carl was eager to duck out after them but Taylor called to him. "Give me a hand, will you, Carl? I want to introduce you to Homer."

The desk clerk began to sweat. "Maybe he's . . . tired. I could come back . . . another time."

"Homer's too wired up to sleep, Carl," Taylor said, chuckling to himself at the joke. His laugh faded as he saw the distressed look on the clerk's face after unfastening the lid of the crate and lifting it up. "Homer doesn't bite, Carl."

"No, sir."

"It's Taylor, remember. Help me get him out. He's not a lightweight."

Carl hesitantly started over, but then froze when he heard a low, masculine voice inside the crate start to sing, "The most beautiful girl in the world..."

The desk clerk gasped, spun around and bolted for the door. "No wonder she left you," he called out. "Maybe she didn't want to stick with a guy who put his pals in crates. Not even for a *fortune*."

Taylor stared in bewilderment at the fleeing desk clerk. And then he burst out laughing. He was laughing so hard he didn't notice that someone new was standing at his open door.

"Homer just tell you a good joke?"

Taylor stopped midlaugh, his eyes darting to the door. "Ali."

Without a word he rushed over to her and pulled her into his arms. For a moment she let her susceptibility show, but then she gathered her common sense about her and she pressed her palms firmly against his chest. "I'm going back to Denver, Taylor. Tonight."

She said it with such finality that Taylor knew there was no use trying to argue her out of her decision.

"Okay. I understand," he said, clipped, impersonal, not understanding at all.

She nodded. *Well, that's that. Now all you've got to do is say goodbye and leave. Make a graceful exit, Ali. Go home and wipe it all from your mind.*

They stood like a pair of cardboard cutouts on opposite sides of a page.

"Goodbye, Taylor."

She spoke so quietly he could scarcely hear the words.

As she started to turn away, his hand shot out. "Aren't you going to tell me to break a leg?"

She nodded, not looking at him, fighting back the tears that threatened, wishing his hand weren't touching her. She took a shaky breath. "Break a leg, Taylor."

His grip tightened. "Last time, you kissed me for good measure."

Her lips quivered. Tears trembled on her lashes. "This time you don't need it. They adore you. They idolize you, Taylor." She smiled crookedly. "'You've come a long way, baby.' You don't need luck. Not when you've got all that *fortune*."

"You're wrong. I do need—" But instead of finishing, he pulled her to him in one swift motion, drawing his mouth down possessively over hers, forcing the invasion of his tongue deep in her mouth.

Ali felt a mix of agony, frustration, anger and longing, yet at the same time she found herself helpless to fight her response to his hard, harsh kiss. She kissed him back with heated urgency, but then pushed herself away. Her "Goodbye" was more a cry as she fled down the hall.

"Isn't she incredible, ladies and gentlemen? Isn't she every man's ideal?" Homer prattled.

Taylor spun around and punched the three-foot robot in the jaw, then immediately gripped his hand in pain. Homer, undented and undaunted, merely broke into song: "The most beautiful girl in the world . . ."

THE MISS INTERNATIONAL pageant was a big production, a show-biz style extravaganza that, this year, in large part thanks to Taylor Fortune, drew record-breaking attendance.

Taylor was in his dressing room, getting ready for his cue to come onstage for the opening of the show. He felt surprisingly calm. Well, perhaps "numb" would have been a more accurate description. For the past week, he'd mechanically gone through the rehearsals, learning his lines, his cues, his marks. Soon after rehearsals got under way, Fiona's flirtatiousness gave way to a well-trained professionalism. After a few days, she'd asked him about Ali. When he told her she'd gone back to Denver, there was real sympathy in Fiona's eyes. It had finally dawned on her that The Fortune Man was hopelessly and most unfortunately in love.

"I hope," she'd said sincerely, "that it wasn't my doing. I didn't mean to make her jealous."

"No," Taylor had assured her. "It was all my doing."

There was a knock on his dressing room door. A moment later, Adam popped his head in. Like Taylor, he was dressed in a tux and looked dashingly handsome. "Come on out for a sec. Everyone wants to wish you luck."

The whole family was out there—his brothers and sisters-in-law, all of whom would be making brief appearances on the show, thanks to Fiona. Jessica and Ben, looking radiantly happy, hands clasped, were there, as well. After everyone wished everyone else good-luck, Jessica followed her grandson back into his dressing room.

She gripped his strong masculine hand in her small, delicate palms. "Are you happy, Taylor?"

He gave her a pained look. "I'm miserable, Gran. I don't like the adulation, the phoniness, the pretension. I don't like the hype, the self-indulgence. I don't like what I've become. I . . . detest The Fortune Man."

She squeezed his hand. "Well, my dear, Ali Spencer got you into this in the first place. It seems only right to me that she figure a way to get you out."

A slow smile came onto his face—the first smile all week. "You're right, Gran. You're absolutely right. There's got to be a way."

Jessica's eyes sparkled. "She's very clever. I'm sure she'll come up with a solution." She started for the door. "She'll be watching you tonight. From her cottage. She phoned me a little while ago...."

"Did she say anything about me? Did she ask you anything about me?"

Jessica smiled. "Not exactly. She told me to tell Homer to break a leg."

WHATEVER ELSE ALI WAS feeling as she watched the Miss International pageant that Saturday night on her small TV up at her cottage, she felt pride. Taylor was doing a slam-bang job as cohost. His delivery was perfect. He was charming, amusing, graceful. And he looked incredibly handsome, practically stealing the show from the newly named Miss International, a willowy brunette from New Zealand. She watched him place a chaste kiss on the new queen's cheek and smile alluringly as he congratulated her. Ali could practically hear every woman in the audience swooning.

Her eyes misted as she experienced a wistful sorrow and a feeling of loss for that shy, clumsy, sweet man Taylor had been when they'd first met. Oh, how she would miss him. Oh, how she loved him....

Her attention had wandered when she was suddenly brought up short by uproarious laughter erupting from the TV. She gasped as she focused on the screen to see Homer accidentally place the shimmering rhinestone-studded crown on Taylor's head instead of Miss International's. As Fiona Jordan stepped in to snatch the crown off his head, she was thunderstruck to find herself caught up in Homer's mechanical clutches. Singing gayly, Homer proceeded to carry the squealing Fiona up the runway with Taylor chasing after them, trying to rescue his cohost from his robot's steely embrace. Meanwhile, poor Miss New Zealand cum Miss International turned bright crimson as she bent down and retrieved the tiara that had fallen off Taylor's head, and crowned herself.

As if there weren't enough pandemonium, Eve Fortune, standing with Adam and the other two Fortune couples at the side of the stage, chose that inopportune moment to go into labor.

THE NEXT DAY AT THE crack of dawn, Ali was jarred from a fitful sleep by strange mournful sounds emanating from outside her secluded cottage. A grizzly bear? A moose? Once fully awake, she realized the sounds were actually melodic. At first she couldn't place the instrument. And then she popped up in bed.

Bagpipes. She was hearing bagpipes.

Flinging off the covers, she raced barefoot across the house and flung open the front door. There, serenading her on the bagpipes, was Taylor. Her hand flew to her mouth. He was even wearing a Scottish kilt.

He stopped playing and gazed with unabashed awe at her in her sheer white cotton nightgown with the wind blowing it against her fine, fine body. "Eve had a baby girl at two this morning," he announced. "I called the hospital from the airplane phone. They're both doing fine."

Ali smiled tremulously. "I'm so happy for them."

After setting his bagpipes down on the ground, Taylor nervously went to shove his trembling hands into his pockets—only there were no pockers in his kilt. So he stretched his hands out toward Ali and gave her a beseeching look. "Oh, Ali. I love you."

Her pulse was drumming all through her body. "I love you, Taylor."

"My grandmother said you got me into this and by rights you should get me out of it."

"I should?"

He stepped toward her. "Yes. And there's only one way you can do it."

Her heart hammered as she watched him approach, looking idiotically wonderful in his kilt, his smile half roguish, half boyishly goofy. Never had she seen a more delicious smile.

"How can I . . . ?" But she couldn't finish the sentence. He was so close now, all words fled from her mind. She closed her eyes, and tears slipped down her cheeks as she felt his arms wrap around her, pulling her close. As he pressed her to him, it was as if the missing piece of herself had finally settled into place.

"There's only one way I can stop being The Fortune Man."

She looked up at him, her wet eyes searching his face. "You don't want to be The Fortune Man anymore?"

"I hate The Fortune Man."

She laughed shakily. "So do I."

He released her suddenly and dropped to the ground on one bare knee, his cheeks flushed but his gaze unwavering, awash with love. "Ali Spencer, you're irresistible. Will you please marry me and make me truly the most fortunate man on earth?"

He was giving up everything for her, but there wasn't an instant's hesitation, a moment's doubt in her mind that this was the right thing to do—for both of them.

"Yes," she whispered, dropping to her knees and flinging her arms around his neck. Taylor lost his balance and they both toppled to the ground.

With a saucy smile, Ali gazed down at his lower body. "I've always been curious about what a Scotsman wore under his kilt."

Epilogue

NOLAN FIELDING chuckled as he read the headlines that morning: The Fortune Man Gains A Bride And Loses A Title—And A Fortune. Still smiling, he set the morning paper aside. It was time to finish getting ready for what the media was billing as the Fortune-brother wedding to beat all Fortune-brother weddings. Which was certainly saying something, as the three preceding events had certainly been far from commonplace. Still, Nolan had no doubt that this wedding would be the topper. And a day of jubilation for all, himself included. Perhaps, he thought, slipping a long white envelope into the inside pocket of his tuxedo jacket, himself most of all.

"NOLAN FIELDING, you look positively gleeful," Doris said, settling into the passenger seat of the attorney's vintage black Bentley sedan.

"And you look positively lovely, Doris," he replied with a wink, taking in her newly coiffed hair, which looked decidedly less gray today, her silk print dress whose scoop neck revealed smooth, creamy and pleasingly taut skin, and her white open-toed pumps, which showed off her slender ankles to great advantage.

Doris blushed. She'd gone out of her way to look her very best today, even letting her hairdresser talk her into a soft brown hair rinse to cover some of the gray. After all, there were some celebrations that were truly once-in-a-lifetime occasions. And there was no doubt that this was one of them.

As the old Bentley neared the Fortune estate, Nolan and Doris could hear helicopters hovering overhead. Doris leaned forward, looking up to see paparazzi hanging from the open chopper doors, filming and snapping shots of the arriving guests.

"Oh, dear, I hope they don't drown out the whole ceremony with that racket," she fretted.

"And just look at this," Nolan said, turning onto the street that led to the property. Both sides of the road were clogged with media vans and passenger vehicles, near which reporters, photographers, tourists, and locals alike crowded around, all hoping to get a glimpse of the select few who held those golden invitations that would allow them through the security-guarded gates.

"You'd think it was a parade," Doris muttered.

Nolan grinned. "No. Just a media circus. It goes with the territory."

"But not for long," Doris pointed out, expecting a confirming nod from her boss.

Instead, Nolan Fielding merely smiled—a most inscrutable smile, at that. Doris eyed him suspiciously. "You look like the cat who swallowed the canary."

Nolan's eyes sparkled. Then he reached into his pocket and pulled out an envelope, handing it over to his faithful secretary. "I suppose, under the circumstances, there should be no secrets between us, Doris. Don't you agree?"

But Doris didn't answer. She was too busy reading. When she was done, she, too, was wearing a smile. A most becoming smile.

NOLAN AND DORIS WERE taken aback to find themselves being led from the house to the rear gardens by that rascal of all robots, Homer. They were both relieved that the mechanical monster was on his best behavior. Doris, however, who had seen the Miss International pageant on TV, was careful to keep her distance, lest she find herself entering the Fortune wedding reception ensnared in Homer's steel clutches.

Both the ceremony and reception were being held in the private gardens behind the main house. Always a favorite spot of Nolan's, with its well-cared-for English-style flower beds and fruit trees, he noticed that the Fortune gardeners had been busy putting in colorful, aromatic tropical plants as well, along with a half-dozen small palm trees for the gala affair. Amid the flowering splendor were groupings of round tables covered in exotic floral-print tablecloths, which were set with elegant china, crystal and silver for the wedding dinner. Off at the far end of the garden, white slatted wooden chairs decorated with colorful floral cushions were set up for the guests on two sides of the mint green carpeted aisle that led to a confectionary white gazebo awash with trumpet honeysuckle.

"It's quite spectacular," Doris murmured breathlessly, so taken aback by the sight that she nearly bumped into Homer, who was doing a rather graceful mechanical pivot for his return trip back to the house to usher in the new arrivals.

"Yes, quite spectacular," Nolan replied, nodding greetings to friends and acquaintances. He started to steer Doris over to the open bar when he saw Jessica and Ben approaching. As always, Nolan was struck by Jessica Fortune's energy and grace, and today, he was especially struck by her radiance. She seemed to sparkle almost as much as the shimmering beads on her teal blue cocktail dress.

Jessica squeezed Doris's shoulder and gave Nolan a peck on the cheek while Ben shook hands with each of them.

"Well," Jessica said brightly, "this does it very nicely, don't you think?"

Nolan smiled awkwardly. "You certainly seem very happy."

"Why shouldn't I be?" Jessica said with élan, linking her arm with Ben's. "I've found the ideal man for me, and all four of my grandsons have found the ideal woman for them. I have one lovely great-granddaughter, and I hope to have a houseful more along the way. And I have no doubt that Taylor will flourish and prosper on his own just as Adam, Peter and Tru have done—thanks in no small part to the Fortune women. Yes, it's all turned out quite well." She squeezed Nolan's hand and gave him a meaningful look. "For all of us."

Nolan's gaze met Doris's for a moment before he nodded faintly.

Jessica laughed softly. "Don't look so uneasy, Nolan. It was my son and not you who came up with that nonsensical tontine in the first place. All's fair in love and business. None of us harbor any ill feelings."

Nolan cleared his throat. "Jessica, I wonder if we—"

"Oh, look, Ben, the Raleighs have arrived. Come, I must introduce you."

Nolan shrugged as he watched Jessica whisk her husband off. Doris laughed gently. "It never was easy for you to get in a word edgewise with that woman."

Nolan chuckled. "And it won't get any easier in the future, I'm sure."

Doris looked around. "There's Adam and Eve and their baby. Don't they look the perfect family? And how fitting that they named their little girl Laura. Laura Ashley Fortune."

Nolan smiled and thought, *Yes, very fitting, indeed.* He eyed the happy couple, thinking back to that day, indelibly etched in his mind, nearly two years ago, when he'd sat with Jessica and the four Fortune boys in his office to read them their father's tontine. Had the possibility even entered his mind at the time that he would end up attending not one but all four of their weddings? Take Adam, the carefree playboy who'd scoffed at the very thought of ever marrying when he was having so much fun being a bachelor. Or straight-arrow Peter, who seemed to eat, sleep and breathe Fortune's, never even making the time for a casual date. Then there was the irascible Tru, who had so little patience with most women, whom he cynically viewed as foolish, silly, and lacking in substance. And last, but most certainly not least, there was the shy, reclusive Taylor with his menagerie of gadgets, who seemed far better matched to his robot than to a flesh-and-blood woman.

Doris gave his sleeve a light tug, shaking him from his reverie. "There're the rest of them," she murmured.

Nolan followed her gaze. Gathered around Adam, Eve and Laura were the rest of the wedding party, save the bride and groom, who wouldn't be making their appearance until the orchestra gathered to play "The Wedding March." Dressed in stunning plum satin off-the-shoulder dresses that matched Eve's, were Sasha and Elizabeth. Ali had chosen the three wives to be her bridesmaids, asking her friend and roommate, Sara, to be her maid of honor. Standing beside their wives were the three celebrated Fortune brothers, all looking dashingly debonair in their white dinner jackets. Since Taylor had refused to single out any one of them, they had decided to all stand up for their baby brother as his best *men*.

"Each of the couples looks so happy," Doris mused. "And so right for each other."

Nolan was surprised and a bit dismayed to find his eyes start to water. "The boys have certainly changed."

For once, Doris didn't scold him for calling them boys. With a gentle smile, she replied, "Love does that to a person. Look at them all now. Adam's become so responsible. Peter's discovered that there's more to life than work. Tru's still the rebel, but with soft edges. And Taylor's come out of his shell with his genuineness and honesty intact."

Nolan felt a lump in his throat as he nodded, agreeing completely with Doris's summations. And finding himself touched by them. Doris discreetly handed him several tissues—one for now and more for the ceremony, which was about to begin.

Somehow, even the sound of the helicopters overhead didn't detract from the hushed anticipation among the guests as the bride, on the arm of her father, a handsome and very proud-looking gray-haired man, started down the aisle.

"Oh, she looks so beautiful," Doris whispered, already sniffing back tears.

Nolan, too, dabbed at his eyes. Each of the Fortune brides had been special and radiant in their own right. He recalled how ethereally lovely Eve had looked on her wedding day, with her Cinderella blond hair, her fine, chiseled features and her Laura Ashley white wedding gown. Elizabeth had made a stunning, statuesque bride, with her flowing auburn hair, her dazzling smile—a woman brimming with confidence, strength, and humor. And then had come Sasha, in a traditional Russian wedding gown that had been her grandmother's and that had brought tears to Jessica's eyes. Sasha had looked so serious, almost somber, walking down the aisle. But as soon as she'd linked hands with Tru, a warm glow had come over her, transforming her, revealing her tenderness and her adventurous spirit.

And now here was Ali Spencer—in just a few minutes Ali Spencer Fortune—with her riot of red curls escaping the slightly lopsided flowered tiara that threatened to slip from her head, trying with only a modicum of success to slow down enough to keep pace with the music. Feisty, spirited Ali, tough and tender in equal measure. Nolan smiled to himself as he watched her join hands with her groom. Yes, he thought, there was no doubt about it. Ali was, as Jessica had said, "Taylor made" for her youngest grandson.

After the ceremony and the joyous, gala reception, when all the other guests and even the helicopters had gone, Nolan Fielding, accompanied by his trusty secretary, Doris, asked the whole family to join him in the library, explaining that there was something he felt compelled to discuss with them without delay.

All four brothers began speaking at once as they stepped into the room, wanting to assure the old lawyer that there were no hard feelings. Nolan gave Doris a quick look and she smiled encouragingly.

"Quiet, boys," Jessica ordered. "Give the poor man a chance to have his say."

Nolan gave Jessica a grateful look as he cleared his throat and stuck his hand inside his jacket pocket and pulled out the white business envelope. Then he searched in his other pockets for his reading glasses.

Doris flicked open her purse and handed them to him.

Again he cleared his throat. Then he looked at the five couples. "Perhaps we could all sit down."

No one was quick to move.

"I think," Doris said quietly, "you'd all do well to be seated."

So they sat, looking questioningly at one another, then focusing their attention on the lawyer with hushed curiosity and anticipation.

With painstaking slowness, Nolan donned his glasses and retrieved a sheet of typewritten paper from the envelope.

"Get on with it, Nolan," Jessica said with her usual impatience, but when Ben reached out and took her hand, she was immediately contrite. "I'm sorry. Curiosity got the best of me for a moment." Ben squeezed her hand.

Nolan smiled at her. "What I have here is an addendum to your son Alexander's codicil."

Everyone stared at Nolan in confusion. "An addendum?" Peter echoed.

"Why are we just finding out about it now?" Tru demanded.

Nolan raised a hand to quiet them. "I was instructed by your father that this envelope could not be opened except under one condition."

"And what condition was that?" Taylor asked quietly.

Nolan looked at all of them and smiled. "That all four of his sons married." He fixed his gaze on each of the Fortune boys in turn. "I asked you in here first to tell you that I will not be taking over the helm of Fortune's." His smile deepened. "I say this with great relief."

"I don't understand," Jessica said. And she was in the majority.

"I think, after I read this letter to you, it will be crystal clear. May I?"

There were unanimous nods.

And so, Nolan Fielding began:

"My dearest family,

"I have long regretted the foolish mistakes I made when it came to love and marriage. I was so cavalier about what should certainly be a sacred institution. I never really gave a thought to the consequences. Indeed, I always felt—foolishly so—that I had nothing to lose. But as you always told me, Mother, if I had chosen wisely, I would have chosen well. If I'd had to search my soul and my pocketbook, I truly believe I would have chosen the one right woman for me. As I watched my four sons grow into manhood, I greatly feared that they would follow in my footsteps. And so, my sons, I devised a

scheme—one that I'm sure none of you met with pleasure. I established the tontine, knowing full well that
with everything at stake, none of you would enter into
a frivolous marriage. I knew that you would weigh your
decision to marry with great care, and that, with your
sage grandmother there to guide you, you would find the
one woman who was right for you. Now that you are all
happily married, I am greatly relieved to tell you that I
never intended, under any circumstances, for the business ever to leave family hands. I know that my dear
friend Nolan will be nothing but relieved to learn that it
is my wish that the stocks that were to revert to him are
instead to be redivided into eight parts, equal portions
going to my four sons and their four wonderful wives.
To all of you, my blessings. And may you all live happily ever after. I have no doubt but that you all will.

> My deepest love,
> Alexander"

By the time Nolan finished reading the letter, there wasn't
a dry eye in the room. Doris passed around tissues. When she
gave one to Jessica, Jessica took hold of the secretary's left
hand.

"Why, Doris!" Jessica exclaimed. "That's an engagement
ring on your finger."

Doris blushed scarlet, her doelike eyes darting to Nolan,
who was also beet red—but smiling happily, nonetheless.
Happily ever after....

HARLEQUIN PRESENTS®

is

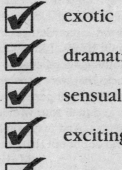

- ✓ exotic
- ✓ dramatic
- ✓ sensual
- ✓ exciting
- ✓ contemporary
- ✓ a fast, involving read
- ✓ terrific!!

*Harlequin Presents—
passionate romances
around the world!*

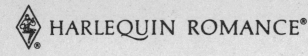

HARLEQUIN ROMANCE®

is

- ☑ contemporary and up-to-date
- ☑ heartwarming
- ☑ romantic
- ☑ exciting
- ☑ involving
- ☑ fresh and delightful
- ☑ a short, satisfying read
- ☑ wonderful!!

Today's Harlequin Romance—the traditional choice!

ROMANCE-Z